25TH AN

The John Morano Eco-Adventure Series

A
WING
AND A
PRAYER

A NOVEL
BY JOHN MORANO

grey gecko press

Text & Illustrations © 2016 by John Morano
Design © 2016 by Grey Gecko Press

All rights reserved. No part of this book may be reproduced or transmitted in
any form or by any means, electronic or mechanical, including photocopying,
recording or by any information storage and retrieval system, without permission
in writing from the publisher. This book is a work of fiction; any resemblance to
real persons (living or dead), events, or entities is purely coincidental.

Published by Grey Gecko Press, Katy, Texas.

www.greygeckopress.com

Printed in the United States of America

Library of Congress Cataloging-in-Publication Data
Morano, John
A wing and a prayer / John Morano
Library of Congress Control Number: 2016942120
ISBN   978-1-9388219-6-7
First Edition

A Wing and a Prayer
is dedicated to Kris:
my blue sky,
my love,
my dream . . .

25ᵗʰ *Anniversary Introduction*

by Mark R. Tercek, President and CEO
The Nature Conservancy

When John Sawhill wrote the introduction to *A Wing and a Prayer* twenty-five years ago, the Nature Conservancy (TNC) had just launched an ambitious campaign. The idea was to raise $300 million to preserve forty of the "Last Great Places" on Earth—wild and pristine areas like the "Islands of Life" in John Morano's wonderful tale, places that rare and threatened species call home.

The campaign was a success—it resulted in the protection of millions of acres in the United States and Latin America. It raised the bar for what TNC and our great partner organizations thought possible in our efforts to protect the Earth's special places.

But fast forward twenty-five years, and we must set that bar even higher.

Don't get me wrong—the environmental movement has a lot to be proud of, from expanded protected areas to government policies that safeguard the air we breathe and the water we drink. Yet every year, the things we want more of—forests, fisheries, healthy soil, coral reefs, biodiversity—continue to decline. And things we want less of, such as carbon pollution that is causing global warming, continue to increase. We need to accelerate and scale up our efforts. But how?

Protect

At TNC, we're very proud of our work to protect important places. That might mean rebuilding an oyster reef, replanting a forest, or restoring a grassland. This work is critical to help stop species like the Guadalupe petrel, which Morano introduces us to in this book, from disappearing.

Take our work on Santa Cruz Island, off the coast of southern California. When TNC purchased the island with the National Park Service in 1978, ten species of plants and animals found nowhere else on Earth—including the Santa Cruz Island fox—were on the brink of extinction. Non-native pigs had attracted golden eagles to the island, which also preyed on the foxes. But intense restoration efforts, including relocating the golden eagles, brought the island back to life. More than 1,200 foxes now live there, up from fewer than 100 in 2004.

Now TNC is taking traditional land protection work like this to a whole new scale, from a recent project that protects millions of acres of forestland in Montana and Washington State to a first-of-its-kind nature preserve in China that is protecting panda habitat and inspiring other similar preserves across the country.

Transform

At the same time, we now realize that buying land to protect it will only get us so far. As we approach a world of nine billion people, one of our newer strategies is helping others reduce their impacts on the environment. With smart science, we are transforming the way businesses, governments, and communities use nature.

For example, in Indonesia, growing demand for palm oil—a common ingredient in our food, cosmetics, soaps, and detergents—is destroying habitat for orangutans, as the rainforest is cut down to make room for palm oil plantations. That's why TNC is teaming up with governments, businesses, communities, and other organizations to find solutions that work for both nature and people.

For example, by working with farmers to produce more palm oil on land that has already been cleared for plantations, we can help prevent additional deforestation—and save crucial orangutan habitat.

Inspire

Perhaps most importantly, we need more people on our side. That's where you come in—and one reason this book is so important.

Through the story of Lupe, John Morano brings to life the connection between our actions and the fate of a species. I hope this book will inspire you to take action to protect the environment.

What can you do? At TNC, we are expanding opportunities for young people to get involved in nature.

If you're a student, gather your classmates and participate in one of our virtual nature field trips or encourage your teacher to explore our other digital education resources. Get involved with volunteer work—like building a school garden or planting trees—to tackle conservation problems in your own community. Or apply for a high school or college internship at an environmental organization. Find out more about ways to get involved with TNC at nature.org/youth.

If you're a parent, uncle or aunt, or teacher, get your kids outside. There's growing evidence that exposure to nature helps children lead happier, healthier lives and helps them excel in school. Not sure where to start? Try getting involved in citizen science projects, many of which you can download on your smartphone. From counting birds near your house to reporting the first time a tulip blooms in your neighborhood, there are lots of ways you can get outdoors and use your observation skills to help scientists collect data about our natural world.

The more we can show people the role that nature plays in all of our lives—clean water and air, protection from storms, flood control, food, enhanced human health and well-being, just to name a few—the better chance we have of saving it. What will drive progress on the environment is compassion, caring about others, and caring about future generations.

Our work today is not just about saving the last great places, but about saving the natural systems all around us—the lands and waters on which all life depends, including the species John Morano gives voice to in his important stories.

Original Introduction

by John C. Sawhill, President and CEO
The Nature Conservancy

A half century ago, pioneering conservationist Aldo Leopold attended the dedication of a small monument marking a great tragedy. Erected by the Wisconsin Society for Ornithology, the monument read, "Dedicated to the last Wisconsin passenger pigeon shot at Babcock, Sept. 1899 – this species became extinct through the avarice and thoughtlessness of man."

As we move into the 21st Century, I often wonder what Leopold would think about the accelerating loss of species that we have witnessed in recent times. No monuments will be built to the losers in the current extinction epidemic; in many cases, species vanish before they have been full described by science. But like the passenger pigeon, each signifies another thread in the web of life that we have eliminated through our careless treatment of the planet in the modern era.

I believe that Leopold would share the chagrin and disappointment of the modern day conservationists at the state of our natural heritage. The fact is, the birds and other animals and plants that represent the wonderful diversity of life on Earth are in serious trouble, and for many of the rarest species, time is running out. Moreover, I think Leopold would see the continuing decline in bird populations as an indication not only of the plight of specific species but also of the troubled condition of our lands and waters.

In *A Wing and a Prayer*, John Morano presents a compelling tale of species extinction as well as an indictment of our mistreatment of the environment. Through his story of a lonely Guadalupe Petrel—a species last seen at the beginning of the 20th Century—he clearly illustrates the obstacles faced by birds at risk. But perhaps more important, *A Wing and a Prayer* also offers us hope: hope that those endangered species struggling to survive have a better than fighting chance. After all, the protected colony of Hawaiian Dark-rumped Petrels that appears in Morano's tale represents a stunningly successful conservation effort.

At high-priority sites around the world, The Nature Conservancy and other conservation organizations are working to protect critical habitat for at-risk animal and plant species. And in particular, by saving habitat for bird species, we hope to ensure the long-term survival of migratory birds, including songbirds, shorebirds, raptors, and waterfowl.

Through the efforts of the Conservancy and others, I strongly believe that we can accomplish lasting conservation results – that we can turn the tide against the kind of species extinction described in *A Wing and a Prayer*. But ultimately, the future of our natural heritage still depends upon people's attitudes about nature, plants, animals – and birds.

While dedicating that Wisconsin monument to the passenger pigeon, Aldo Leopold noted that people must achieve "a sense of community with living things, and of wonder over the magnitude and duration of the biotic enterprise." Until we fully understand and embrace our close connection to the natural world, the fate of magical creatures such as the Petrel remains imperiled.

Part One

A Bird in the Hand

For Lupé, the day began like every other day, with the mindless flick of a finger followed by instant light from a long thin sun that did not warm or move. This did not compare to the slow rise of Pettr's glowing eye, the eye that watched over the planet and every morning rinsed the night from the sky.

The sunrise Lupé remembered was anything but silent and quick. It sang with the songs of thousands of birds and the constant *crash-swish*, *crash-swish* of the steady surf. The sunrise of Lupé's freedom was a slow, deliberate celebration of life, a beautiful beginning to each new day. This wonderful memory, however, had been interrupted by the cold reality of a painful captivity.

Lupé was a prisoner, held in what he believed was a hard silver web spun by the man-flock. Although it was large enough for him to stretch and pace, flight was impossible. So he sat, remembered what it was like to be free, and waited for a sign from his savior, Pettr.

Lupé was a very proud petrel, and like most petrels, he worshipped Pettr, the Creator, the first to walk on water. However, it wasn't being a petrel that made Lupé special, for there were many living on the planet. What made him special was his flock—the Gwattas—and the very real possibility that he might be the last of their kind. And that is precisely why the man-flock held him.

Even so, Lupé saw no sense in his captivity but realized that this was typical of the man-flock. No other creature was given more power with less knowledge. "Why did Pettr create them at all?" he wondered.

The petrel knew he must find a female of his flock somewhere on the planet and mate with her before either of them perished. Unfortunately, there were two problems with this solution: the man-flock physically prevented him from conducting his search, and he was not sure if there was a female from his flock still alive. As far as he was concerned, all his confinement did was waste valuable time, since he knew he would not live forever.

The petrel was tortured with the thought that he might not fulfill his quest, that his species would die with him locked in the silver web of the man-flock. One way or another, he was determined to escape. And he prayed to Pettr to help show him the way.

For a moment, Lupé drifted back to the day he was plucked from the Earth like a minnow from the sea. He had been standing on a rock, deciding whether to sleep or fish, when he had heard the sound he thought he might go his entire life without hearing: the call of a female from his flock. Every muscle in his body had tensed as he had tried to catch her scent.

For some reason, the wind would not deliver the sweet smell to his beak, yet he could still hear her faint calling. Carried by small, powerful wings, the petrel flew toward the confusing caw.

As her call became clearer, Lupé noticed a crevice between two huge rocks. The throaty purr of the female came from deep within. It occurred to Lupé that this would have been a wonderful nesting site had the man-flock not left their rodents and cats on the island.

The petrel began an ancient song he had never sung before, the mating song born within him that could save the Gwattas.

Still, the female quietly called.

"Why does she not join in the sacred verse?" Lupé questioned. "Is she hurt?" Then he wondered whether he was singing the song correctly. Whatever the reason for her reluctance, Lupé knew he couldn't let her get away. He flew into the crevice prepared to meet the future of his flock and prepared to battle any who threatened her.

Suddenly, there was a loud *pop*. Lupé was tangled and bound. His tiny body flailed and convulsed. The more he fought, the tighter he was held. He struggled so viciously, he felt his wing tear from his flank. Soon he was covered with his own warm blood, the precious blood of an entire species. Then he felt them for the first time, those disgusting featherless fingers of the man-flock.

They held him firmly and snapped a silver ring around his ankle to match the empty silver web they had waiting for him on the other side of the planet. The female he had flown to was nothing more than an empty voice, a trick of the man-flock. Lupé was taken from his home.

As the petrel's memory faded, he returned to the reality of the moment and wondered why the man-flock would want to hold him. If they wanted to ensure the extinction of his flock, why not kill him? If they wanted to help, why not release him and allow him to continue his search? This torture, this cruelty, made no sense.

Lupé thought, *They cannot learn anything from me like this. I am kept. What they see before them is not a petrel . . . I am the Earth, and it is me. We define each other. I am not merely feather and bone, but ocean and sky as well. It is only among my friends, the wind and the water, that I can be understood . . . The petrel does not sit, it soars.*

Every so often, one of the man-flock would remove Lupé and clip feathers from his wings. For any bird, this would be the ultimate humiliation. It was especially true for Lupé, who believed he could fly like no other. The petrel was proud of his dark plumage that enabled him to blend in with the deep water and the lava-stone islands of his origin. His pale underside and white chest helped him disappear against the clouds and the surf. Sitting inside the shiny silver web, Lupé looked like a shadow of himself, dark and quiet.

Suffering the humiliation of having his wings clipped, combined with the revulsion of being held by those fingers, provided Lupé with two more reasons to plot his escape.

While he was sitting quietly in a place he would rather not be, a hand would invade and grasp him, preventing him from moving. He would be removed momentarily while another hand pulled his wing from his flank and stretched it. Feathers would be eliminated, cut down to the skin so that flight fell away with the quills.

The petrel was subjected to the indignity randomly, at the whim of his captors. Ironically, it was the clipping, an act intended to keep him where he was, that led to the first phase of his plan to get away.

If Lupé was the sole survivor of his species, it was not because he was a coward or because he was stupid. Lupé had survived because he was fearless and cunning. Had the flock been tasked to select a single petrel to continue their line, Lupé would have been a solid choice. He began to form his plan.

The petrel decided that no matter what happened, if he wanted to escape, he'd have to be able to fly. Also, he assumed that because he was still alive, the man-flock wanted him to stay that way. He would not allow his wings to be clipped anymore. He decided that he would be killed before he was snipped again. Faced with the death of their prisoner, perhaps the man-flock would abandon the practice of docking his wings.

The next time the featherless hand reached into the silver web, Lupé went wild, pecking, flapping, thrashing, and spitting sticky, hot oil through a short tube on the top of his beak. Lupé had no regard for himself as he tried to tear the flesh from the hand. He even reinjured his wing during the protest. Although it was really a minor wound, the petrel was aware that in the wild, any injury could have fatal results.

Damaged and bloody, Lupé lost the battle with the man-flock, but he hoped he had won the war. If it was the last time his captors attempted to clip his wings, then once his feathers grew back, should the opportunity present itself, he would be able to fly to freedom.

For the most part, Lupé spent his days doing two things: praying to Pettr and staring at the sky through a strange opening just above him that was clear, yet sealed. At first, Lupé was confused by the sight of the open sky. He didn't know what to make of it. He could see the clouds, but he could not feel the wind, taste the rain, or touch what was out there.

After a while, he believed he had figured it all out. He decided that the opening was covered by the frozen water he had seen during his travels to the cold seas. How the man-flock managed to keep it frozen, even when it was warm outside, he could not say. Nothing passed through the opening, but he could see what was on the other side, the side he wanted to be on.

Outside, the petrel saw a tall tree with many branches. One of the limbs reached right up to the opening. When the breeze blew, Lupé could occasionally hear the branch tap against it. He enjoyed listening to the gentle beat that moved with the rhythm of the wind. The sound enabled him to imagine the subtle shifts and tremors of the old friend who carried him in flight.

Lupé tried to relive the sensation of the wind blowing through his feathers, carrying him to the deep water to feed until he was full. Then his friend would help ferry him home to the island of his flock, where Lupé would thank both the wind and Pettr for taking such good care of him.

Mostly, Lupé missed the fragrance of the sea, the touch of the rocky earth, and the call of the breeze. Having his senses and feelings contained was one of the most painful parts of his captivity. Every aspect of the petrel's being was locked up except for one, his desire to be free. Although he couldn't see or feel the wind through the opening, he knew it was out there calling him, waiting for him.

In a sense, Lupé's view of the strange opening paralleled what his flock thought of the sun. They believed the sun was actually the eye of the Lord, Pettr. Everything on the planet, the Earth itself, was contained inside God's body. Everything they encountered was physically part of the Creator.

This was one of the reasons why the petrels could not understand the destruction the man-flock subjected the planet to. They saw it as an attack on the actual body of God. While it was hard for them to accept this behavior, because the birds knew that the man-flock was injuring their Lord, the petrels prayed that Pettr's reprisals would not harm them as well.

They were terrified of the strange new rain that burned their eyes and singed the planet, gradually making the sea itself more acidic. They called it "Pettr's tears" and believed that if these tears continued to fall, they would wash away whatever was harming the planet. The birds hoped that they would not be swept away as well and worried what the effect would be on the others who were not part of the man-flock or their ways.

Lupé had also been taught an interesting view of death. He believed that in order for a bird to get to heaven, it must "fly the good flight" while it lived, being true to Pettr and the planet. Any bird that accomplished this and died would be able to fly to the sun, pass through Pettr's eye, and join their Lord on the other side, the side where the many flew as one.

Those who were false, who had not flown the good flight, would burn when they tried to pass through the sun. Only those who had given their best to the world would be permitted to fly through Pettr's eye unharmed.

Lupé prayed that someday, Pettr would allow him to pass through the opening beyond the web so that he could experience heaven on Earth, freedom.

One of the greatest privileges of being free was feeding. As a captive, Lupé was tormented at being fed. No doubt the man-flock thought they were taking great care of their "guest," but that was not the case. Actually, they couldn't have been more cruel or insulting.

The limp, lifeless pieces of shrimp, squid, and clam that were cleaned, cut, and laid before him did not truly nourish or satisfy him. Feeding was a spiritual act, and Lupé's spirit was being starved. The food he was given was too clean. It was sterile, expired, and frozen. It was cold, frosty, neither warm nor vital. It was laid out in colorful shells created by the man-flock. This was not feeding.

Lupé was robbed of the ritual of gathering his own meal. For a petrel, ingesting was only a small part of eating. The flight, the search, the acquisition, the return, and the thanks were all equally important parts of the whole. One needed cunning, strength, and skill to feed.

Among the man-flock, one only needed to bend over, to bow to the captors in order to eat. Lupé was further insulted because only petrel chicks and those who are too old or feeble were fed by others. A full-grown petrel only accepted a meal offered from the ocean, one he gathered himself.

Disgusted at what lay in front of him, Lupé reminded himself, "I am of the deep water and the open sky. I eat the little fish. And I have never eaten the scraps from the tiny islands the man-flock floats on the ocean." Yet he choked the morsels down, understanding, perhaps better than the man-flock, he needed to survive even if doing so was, at the moment, distasteful.

Whenever Lupé's meal arrived, he would mentally transport himself to the islands and try to relive his feeding ritual. Captured but not contained, Lupé would release his mind, allowing it to soar off until he was alone in a cloudless sky, floating silently above the ocean, carefully watching the water below. Inevitably, a reef of dancing shrimp would appear, the water thick with the little fishes hopping and popping just above the surface of the sea.

Circling, Lupé would open his beak, taste the salt in the wet air, and then dive toward the meal. Pulling up at the last second, he would level himself and walk on the water, skimming his beak through the massive school, filling it with choice morsels. It was as if the ocean squeezed the fish out of the sea just to feed him. Lupé would eat until he was satisfied, then return to the clouds where he would thank Pettr and fly home fulfilled.

For any petrel, this was one of the most sacred experiences of life, second only to mating. It sustained them physically and spiritually, but what the man-flock offered Lupé was something less than scavenging, a painful insult. So when he was completely absorbed in his vision, Lupé would close his eyes tightly and force himself to eat what was in front of him, pretending all the while that he was home, feeding in the deep water.

Although Lupé was not nearly as religious as some birds, he did spend much of his time meditating and praying. Actually, there wasn't much else for him to do, and Lupé was convinced Pettr would help him escape if he could only reach him through prayer.

The petrel recalled that most flocks of sea birds had individual members known as "birds of pray." Lupé's flock called them "savns." They were almost always found by the shore, facing into the wind, meditating. Indeed, Lupé's grandmother, Pakeet, was a legendary savn. As a youngster, he had always felt a quiet presence whenever he was around either Pakeet or his mother, Raza.

It was said that the birds of pray spoke directly to Pettr. Lupé wasn't sure if this was true or not, but he had seen them change the weather on several occasions. On cloudy, rainy days, the birds would pray—alone or in groups—for Pettr's eye to reappear in the sky.

As they silently recited their individual mantra over and over, the rain would cease, the clouds would pass, the sea would calm, and the sun would emerge, bright and beautiful, to dry damp feathers.

How these birds spoke to Pettr was still a mystery to Lupé, although he did speak to a blue booby named Beako once who tried to explain. Beako told Lupé that all sea birds who meditated did the same thing. They sat facing into the breeze because it was the only

way the wind could speak to them. They sat near the shore so the ocean could add its message.

In their minds, the birds would silently chant an ancient mantra. This would unite the voices of the wind, the ocean, and the Earth, revealing one very special voice, Pettr's. Having reached this plateau, the birds of pray would be able to speak directly with their Lord.

As a very young petrel, Lupé remembered following his grandmother to the shore. He knew she was a special bird, and he wanted to see why the other birds treated her with so much respect. He watched Pakeet as she stood only a flap or two from the shore and turned to face the wind. The youngster stood behind his grandmother and did exactly as she did. He stood there listening, waiting, and watching . . . Then he fell asleep.

When he awoke, Pakeet was standing over him. He had slept for the entire day while his grandmother prayed. She asked him if he had a good sleep. Then she inquired, "What is it you prayed for, Lupé?"

After a moment's thought, the petrel said, "I prayed for a brother, but Pettr didn't hear me."

"How do you know what Pettr hears?" she asked.

"I know he didn't hear me because I don't pray very well . . . I get distracted. My mind wanders, and I fall asleep."

"If you believe in what you pray for, that is enough to get Pettr's attention . . . Did you dream?" Pakeet questioned.

"Yes, let me think . . . I dreamt about another who looked just like me, a female. Not a brother. We were together on a different island . . . and you were there. But it was just a dream. I've had it before. It's not important," Lupé said.

Pakeet raised the feathers on the back of her neck as she often did when she was thinking. Then she said, "Maybe the dream is nothing . . . but maybe the dream is an answer from Pettr. Maybe he is telling you that he hears your prayers, that you will have a sister, or that some other female will come to you one day."

While Lupé thought this over, his grandmother motioned him closer. She looked around to make sure they were alone, and then she said, "I can help you stay awake when you pray, Lupé."

The young bird listened carefully as his grandmother continued.

"There are certain words that savns like me say over and over while we pray. I cannot tell you all of them, but Pettr would not mind if I told you your first word. Should you fly the good flight throughout your life, you might just find out what your other words are . . . For now, whenever you pray, repeat the word '*Sea*' over and over. Picture it. Smell it. Hear it. Be one with it, and your prayers will be stronger."

Lupé remembered the conversation with his grandmother vividly. If ever there was a time to put her advice to the test, it was now. So he decided he would try to recreate the savn's conditions inside the silver web. Perhaps he could find another word of his mantra. But there were many problems to overcome.

To begin with, Lupé was not near the ocean. The only thing remotely like the sea was a hollow silver branch that fresh water flowed from when the man-flock touched it. And there was no wind, at least no wind that Lupé had spoken with before. There was, however, a cool, stale breeze that always blew with the same force in the same direction, but only when it was warm and the man-flock was about. Like the water from the silver branch, this wind had no voice. It continuously moaned the same lifeless sound.

Looking at the problems that faced him, Lupé thought his chances of speaking to Pettr were slim. He chose to try anyway. So he prayed . . . and nothing happened.

Later that same day, while Lupé daydreamed as he looked out at the sky through the opening, he noticed that a pair of robins nesting on a branch nearest him had laid an egg. Usually, Lupé paid no attention to nests and eggs. They only depressed him, making him wonder if he would ever father his own chicks. The only reason this nest interested him at all was that both the mother and the father were nowhere to be found. They had left their lovely blue egg completely unattended. At least one parent would usually remain with the egg at all times. Lupé knew if he ever had young, he would take better care of them.

As he continued to watch, Lupé realized he was mistaken. The egg was not entirely abandoned. A very old butterfly, colored in orange and black, sat on it. Lupé found this very funny, because the butterfly's rear end covered only a fraction of the egg. Was the butterfly tasting it? Lupé wondered. He had been told that these insects taste their meals through their feet. Was he trying to incubate the egg? There was no way the little insect could warm the orb, or protect it for that matter.

So, for the first time since his capture, Lupé laughed, amused at the absurdity of the situation. Even though the butterfly could not hear the petrel sputtering, he turned toward Lupé and smiled. Then he sat down even harder on the egg as if to say, "Laugh if you will, but if I choose to sit on an egg, then that's exactly what I'm going to do."

Beyond the nest, silhouetted against a distant cloud, Lupé saw the returning mother. As she bent her wings and began to dive, Lupé knew what she had in mind for the old butterfly sitting harmlessly atop the egg. For a moment, Lupé was stunned, not knowing what to do.

He didn't want to see his little friend die, so he began to hop up and down and flap his wings, hoping the butterfly would get the message. He didn't. The old egg-sitter just stayed where he was, stubbornly flashing his huge grin at Lupé. He was probably enjoying the petrel's performance.

At the last second, just before the angry mother was about to swallow the butterfly, Lupé pushed out a piercing caw, one that would have made any petrel proud. Following Lupé's cue, all the other creatures being held captive by the man-flock began to whistle, peep, squeak, hoot, and screech. The butterfly just kept smiling and casually drew his wings together, as if to stretch. He made no motion to leave the egg. Then it was too late.

The robin was on the nest and ready to make her kill when the butterfly . . . disappeared. It didn't fly away. It simply vanished. While the mother robin pecked at the empty air around the nest, Lupé wondered whether he was seeing things, if captivity had finally affected his mind.

Whenever Lupé thought about protecting eggs or young, the word "rat" came to mind. If there was one creature the petrel hated above all others, even the man-flock, it was the rat. Rodents were the vermin mainly responsible for devastating Lupé's flock and family. They ate the young, the old, and the unhatched.

Lupé was also convinced that at night, a large rat roamed outside the silver web. The petrel was very concerned about this. He had fought rats before and won, but never like this, never without the use of flight. Also, he had a feeling that the rat who roamed the area around the web was a rather large, hungry rodent, perhaps larger, hungrier than any he encountered before.

Lupé had suspected its presence since his arrival long ago, but lately, the rat was growing bolder, coming closer. Because it made him feel ill, Lupé hadn't been eating all the food the man-flock provided. He knew this was a mistake; the scraps would attract the hairy scavenger.

Still, there was something very puzzling about all of this. Lupé never actually saw the rodent, nor could he find physical evidence of the dirty visitor. He was sure he had heard and smelt him several times, but in the morning, there were no footprints, no hairs, no droppings anywhere to be found. This was obviously a very clever rodent—one more reason why Lupé had to worry. The petrel had a feeling that tonight, he would find out how clever this rat was and how well he could protect himself while contained in a small space. It was not something Lupé looked forward to.

The more he thought about the rat, the more determined Lupé was to defend himself. He remembered how rats had killed all the birds of his family, how they had raided the nests and devoured the future of the Gwattas until he was all that remained. The burrowing petrels had had no defense against the rodents the man-flock had left behind when they visited the islands.

Many of the mature birds could survive the onslaught, but as the eggs were systematically consumed, no new generations had emerged to replace the elders who flew to Pettr. In three generations, virtually all of his flock were killed. Lupé's beak tightened, and his feathers tensed. The images of death would not go away.

Once again, the petrel began to drift back to Gwatta, the island of his youth. Many had already perished. Lupé and his parents, Kurah and Raza, lived together on bare rock under the ledge of a boulder only a few flaps from shore. It was a good nesting site, and no petrel would dare challenge Kurah for the location between the rocks. But no one was safe from the rats roaming the island.

A young bird at the time, Lupé had been flying for only a short while. One day in particular, he sat on the rocky ledge so that he could protect his younger brother, Barau, who was only a few days away from the greatest moment in any bird's life: first flight. For the first time since Raza had borne the egg that had become Barau, she and Kurah had left the nest to fish together. Lupé watched over his brother and scanned the sky for his parents' return.

Chicks were not usually named until they flew from the nest, but Lupé had been so happy at the idea of having a brother, he couldn't wait to name him. According to the birds of Lupé's flock, Barau meant "friend of the sea." Lupé had hoped the name would give his brother luck when fishing. Barau returned his brother's love and hoped that someday soon, they would fly and fish together.

It was a frightening thing for a young bird—any bird, for that matter—not to be able to fly, especially with his parents gone, so on that day, Barau peeped to his brother constantly. Every time he was called, Lupé glided down from the ledge that overlooked the shore to reassure his brother with mellow hooting and a gentle peck. But as the morning wore on, Lupé grew hungry and restless.

He could hear the surf and the wind teasing, which only added to his impatience.

After a while, Barau began to complain that he, too, was hungry. The youngster had not eaten much solid food, so Lupé thought he'd offer his brother a treat. He said, "Barau, how would you like to share some nice, fresh crab meat with me?"

Barau's eyes lit with excitement as he squeaked, "Do you think I'm ready to eat some?"

"Of course you are," Lupé said. "I'll find a nice, big crab and fly overhead. Then I'll drop it down on the rocks right here and we can eat together."

Little Barau glowed. "Yes, yes!"

Lupé told him to lie down against the rocks under the ledge until he returned with the crab. He warned his brother that even though his coloring concealed him, unnecessary movement would expose him. Looking back, Lupé could barely see Barau's gray body snuggled among the dull rocks, but there was no mistaking the sound of the youngster's happy peeping as his older brother flew toward the beach in search of a treat.

While scanning the shore for a good-sized crab, Lupé encountered a pair of petrels from his own flock, Bax and Stee-sky. They were not much older than him. It was a time when Lupé rarely saw others so much like himself. He was overjoyed and decided to spend some time with his two new friends. The three dropped clams on the rocks, splashed in the surf, and played tag in the clouds—all the things that young petrels should do together.

Soon, the wind began to shake Lupé. It tugged at his feathers and reminded him of Barau. Lupé felt a strange sensation in his breast. The wind warned that something terrible was happening. The petrel flew to his brother.

When Lupé returned to the nest he saw a sight he would never forget. A rat had killed Barau, eaten him from the neck down. The little bird's body was torn open and cleaned out like an empty shell on the beach, two halves, lifeless and stiff. Lupé stared at the fluffy down strewn among the rocks. The tiny feathers that had been almost ready for flight were covered with Barau's blood. Lupé could not quiet the image of his grounded brother pinned to the rocks, powerless to escape the ravenous rodent.

When Kurah and Raza arrived, no words were exchanged. They blamed themselves, not Lupé, for the loss of Barau. Silently, they cleaned and prepared their roost for another chick, who never came.

Lupé viewed the prospect of facing a rat in the evening as an opportunity to avenge Barau's death, but deep down, he knew the death of a rodent would not give his brother final rest. Barau's death could only be avenged by birth, not by more killing. The only fitting tribute for Barau and the others who had been killed by the rodents would be the continuance of the flock. Nevertheless, Lupé readied himself for whatever the night delivered.

The petrel gazed through the opening. Beyond the robin's nest, he saw a bright full moon watching over him, and he felt he was not alone. On nights of the full moon, Pettr extended his watch over the planet. This night would be blessed with the light of the moon and would enable Lupé to clearly see his foe. He believed Pettr would protect him tonight and deliver his flock from extinction by helping him survive. He just didn't know how any of that was going to happen.

Looking back at the moon, Lupé imagined that if there was a female for him out there somewhere and she was looking up at this very moment, she would see the same moon. Although they hadn't found each other, Lupé was comforted by the thought that they could share this vision.

Then he said to himself, "Tonight, the moon is a female, a beautiful female feathered in white and gray, just like me. She is not of my flock, but she is pure, and we have found each other. Tonight, the moon will be my mate, my love, my dream." Lupé thanked Pettr for the vision and fell fast asleep, pretending, at least for a moment, that he had found what he was looking for.

A sound whipped the petrel from his sleep. In an instant, he knew that shuffling, smelly rat was about. He sensed the rodent more clearly tonight. He imagined the teeth and the small, sharp claws. He remembered what they were capable of. He remembered the sight of Barau and readied himself. He puffed his feathers. It made him look larger than he was. He coiled his neck, lowered his beak, and waited. There was no telltale sniffling or squeaking, but there was that incessant rustling, the disgusting shuffle of dirty feet that never left the ground. And they were coming closer.

Lupé had come across a few birds who believed that one died because it was one's time. Somewhat resigned to their "fate," they might do less to challenge their demise. He thought, *If they are correct, my best efforts won't save me . . . but if they are wrong, my best efforts just might save me.* He decided that he would never assume it was his time to die. He would always fight to force Pettr to prove that it was time for him to fly to the sun.

Suddenly, a shadow moved along a wall lit by the moon. The figure had a rigid, thin tail trailing behind it. Its middle was thick, even for a rat. The neck was long and slender, with a small, pointed snout at the tip. The rodent seemed to waddle as it scurried between the shadows of the night. Lupé wondered if it was old or had injured a leg. No matter; it moved with stealth and cunning. This was dangerous. A large rat that could move like this was something to be feared, especially when one was trapped in the silver web of the man-flock.

Before Lupé could move a muscle, the rodent poked its head through the hard web and grabbed a small chunk of fish. There was only one creature on the face of the Earth Lupé would not share his food with: this one. The petrel waited for the rodent to go after another morsel. He knew from experience that rats do not stop eating when they are full: they eat until there is no food left, so this rodent would return. Lupé decided that the next time the rat exposed its tiny, smelly head, he would drive his beak into the scavenger's neck or skull and then twist with all his might.

Now the rodent was behind Lupé, grabbing another scrap. *When the scraps are gone, will I be next?* the petrel wondered. Not waiting for an answer, Lupé turned and attacked. He threw himself at the dark shadow behind him. The silver web deflected the bird's beak with a clank, and the rodent scurried back into the night.

Lupé thought for a moment, then pushed a larger piece of shrimp halfway through the web to tempt his target. When the rat stepped up and began to tear at it, Lupé shot a stream of sticky, hot oil in the thief's face, just as he had done when the man-flock had tried to clip his wings. The rodent screamed and ran.

The scream puzzled the petrel. It was a scream unlike any noise he had ever heard a rodent make. And where the piece of shrimp was left, small, gray feathers remained. There were several, all very short and covered with dirt. Lupé wondered if the rodent had killed a hatchling earlier in the evening. The man-flock had many to choose from. The thought of the rodent slaughtering chicks only made the petrel more intent on punishing the vermin.

As Lupé tried to plan his next course of action, he heard a low crying. It wasn't the wail of physical pain; rather, it was the soft cooing of hurt feelings. *Is this a trick or another victim of the rat?* he wondered. All he could do was ready himself for the next encounter.

Out of the shadows and into the moonlight waddled a chubby, dirty, sobbing pigeon. The pigeon rubbed its eyes with a twisted wing. Foul-smelling orange oil dripped from its head and tiny beak. Beneath the tears, the pigeon was muttering something. It said, "I'm sorry . . . I really am . . . If you wanted your food, why didn't you eat it? To offer me such a nice piece and then cover me with hot oil, that's not very friendly."

"Shhh," Lupé said. "Be quiet. There's a rat loose tonight, and I cannot help you from in here."

"Very funny," the filthy pigeon replied. "Now you're going to insult me just because I happen to be a rat."

It dawned on the petrel that for some reason this . . . pigeon believed it was a rat. Not only did it look, smell, and act like one, but it even spoke like a rat. It mumbled and squeaked its words so fast, Lupé had to strain to understand it. Finally, Lupé realized he was dealing with a pigeon that had a few loose feathers.

"I apologize if I hurt you," the petrel said, "but I didn't know you were of the feather and the wing . . ."

"You're making fun of me again!" the chubby pigeon shouted. "I am as fine a rodent as ever scurried across the flesh of this planet. I thank my maker every day that I am not some web-footed, feather-covered failure like you . . . Now, are we going to be friends or not? I will not be insulted again."

This bird's out of its tree, Lupé thought. But he decided that having a friend on the outside, even a loony one, would not be such a terrible thing. He asked, "What is your name, strange . . . rodent?"

The rat-bird replied, "My name is Zomis. And what is your name?"

"I am Lupé."

All this time, Zomis barely even looked at Lupé. Its stare was fixed upon the scraps at the feet of the new acquaintance.

The petrel got the message immediately and shoved a few chunks of squid in the direction of Zomis, who began to eat them even before they were through the silver web.

Like most rodents, Zomis conversed while chewing—pecking, actually. "I've never seen a bird like you. Are you some type of gull?"

"I am a petrel."

Zomis continued, "But you are rare. You are here because you have very few cousins, yes?"

Lupé nodded. He decided he would not tell Zomis anything he did not have to until he was sure Zomis could be relied upon. The petrel realized that for a bird baffled by its own identity, Zomis could be very sharp about other things. This could be a danger, but if Lupé was careful, it might be something he could use to escape.

It was obvious having been held by the man-flock earlier in its life had a strange effect on Zomis. The portion of the pigeon's character that was still bird and not rat explained to Lupé that many of its kind—it claimed a single flock could number more than a billion birds—had also been killed by rodents but pointed out that the flock had mainly been eliminated by humans.

Lupé didn't doubt that the man-flock could eradicate the species, but he had a hard time imagining a single flock of a billion pigeons. He would have to be careful processing information from Zomis.

Ultimately, rather than feel the hatred of rodents that Lupé felt, Zomis had chosen to become one.

At first, it wasn't very easy for Lupé to associate with the rat-bird. There was too much about the creature that reminded Lupé of real rodents, but it had been a long time since he had had someone to talk to.Once he managed to ignore Zomis's rat-like qualities, he actually enjoyed chatting the night away with his new friend. He suspected that beneath all the blubber and grime, Zomis was nothing more than a pleasant, mixed-up pigeon. Lupé even began eating better, now that feeding had become more of a social event.

"I was also captured by the man-flock, probably for the same reason they took you," Zomis explained. "But I slipped away, and they forgot about me. They have no interest in rats."

The petrel wondered whether the pigeon was telling the truth. More importantly, he wondered just how his new friend managed to "slip away."

Zomis looked so much like a rat, it was tough to tell just what flock the pigeon belonged to. Even its gender was a mystery. Under the grime, there seemed to be delicate feathers of slate and gray with touches of blue. The short, sharp beak was black, as were Zomis's eyes. The coloring of the stout rat-bird was not all that different from Lupé himself. Still, the petrel couldn't tell whether Zomis was an ordinary pigeon or a vital part of a rare breed. Either way, it really didn't matter to Lupé; he had problems of his own to work out.

The petrel had seen birds fly with different flocks. Indeed, it was common. He remembered quite a few pelican and gull friends who had mingled with his flock. Some of the more feather-brained occasionally forgot what flock they belonged to. Lupé smiled at the memory of a pelican named Pinny who believed he was of the woodpecker flock.

It was quite a sight to see, the enormous pelican flying with birds only a fraction of his size. His beak alone was as big as an entire woodpecker. Landing on a small branch with the rest of his adopted flock, Pinny would slip and slide as he tried to grip the tiny stick with his webbed feet. But the funniest sight of all was seeing the confused bird peck at the tree with his massive, dull beak. The pelican never managed to attain the staccato rapping the other woodpeckers performed quite effortlessly. But that's not to suggest that Pinny didn't possess talent and determination.

Without even seeing him, you knew when Pinny was working on a tree. Half the island would echo with the distinctive *whap, whap, whap* of the pelican's blunt beak slamming against a tree trunk. Pinny usually managed only three or four blasts before he became dizzy and slipped completely off the branch.

Even though Pinny's mind was as slow as the tide, after a few shattering headaches and one or two crash landings, the pelican realized he would be better off with his own flock, although he did remain very friendly with the woodpeckers. So, never in his life had Lupé met a bird that actually forgot it was a bird—not until Zomis, that is. For Lupé, the idea of denying one's identity as a bird was unthinkable.

All things considered, Zomis had done a remarkable job of concealing the fact that it was a bird. There was, however, one thing that Zomis could not hide no matter how hard it tried—its weight. Zomis was large. In fact, the rat-bird was so plump that Lupé could not imagine the dirty pigeon being physically able to fly. This upset Lupé. He was taught to believe that the most sacred endowment Pettr could bestow upon a creature was the ability to fly. To reject this gift was to say no to God.

One morning, as the first rays of sunlight penetrated the opening and fell upon the two birds, Zomis gobbled up a piece of dried shrimp it was pecking at and quickly waddled toward its hole in the wall. The rat-bird's feathers, slick with dirt, shook in unison with the layers of flab beneath them.

Zomis turned to Lupé and said, "I'll see you tonight. You know, for a bird, you're not half bad . . . And don't forget to save me some scallops." Then the petrel's friend muttered, "I love the scallops. They're sooo tasty. Ah, but that squid is good too. Oh, and those shrimp . . ."

Lupé laughed at what a sponge his pal could be as the sputtering Zomis disappeared into the hole in the wall. The petrel amused himself with the thought that either the hole would have to get bigger or Zomis would have to get smaller. He knew the odds were with the hole.

Soon after Zomis's exit, the long, thin sun that never warmed or moved flashed its white light. Then the dead wind began to blow. It meant the man-flock had arrived. Another day had begun. Lupé watched several of the man-flock as they gathered in a corner, drawn to a strange bouncing light in a burrow. Like most things that had to do with the man-flock, Lupé didn't understand the strange light or their fascination with it. Deep inside the dark square, there was light, movement, and sound.

The man-flock listened very carefully to the voices from the burrow. Lupé believed it must be part of their religion, if they had any. He wondered if the noisy light helped them speak to their God the way the wind and the sea helped him speak to Pettr. The power it seemed to hold over his captors frightened him. Lupé considered whether the light in the burrow could command the man-flock to release him. When they were not around, Lupé would try to speak to the strange light, to reason with it. It might be smarter than the man-flock.

No matter how bleak things appeared, Lupé devoted himself to three ideas: hope that he would escape, faith in Pettr, and love for the female he knew he would find one day. On the islands of his youth, it was very easy to pray. The wind and the ocean were still very much alive. Sincere prayers were carried to Pettr, and sometimes the Creator's own words were returned. To the more devoted birds of pray—the savns—the wind, the sea, and the Earth revealed the secrets of the planet, the secrets of life and death.

Praying in the silver web was difficult. Lupé didn't understand the language of the strange dead wind, but it was all he had. So the petrel stood on one leg—a prayer posture he had learned from Pakeet—faced into the queer breeze, and began to pray for the survival of his race, hoping all the while that Pettr would hear him through the web.

While Lupé communed, water began to flow from the hollow silver branch near the ledge where the petrel was contained. Water always seemed to flow and light always seemed to shine when the man-flock needed it.

Several words, very faint, echoed in the distant burrows of Lupé's mind. The petrel slammed his eyes shut and tried to transport himself back to the islands. He repeated the first word of the savns's mantra over and over, just the way his grandmother showed him so long ago: "*Sea . . . sea . . . sea . . . sea.*" The other words grew louder, but still he could not hear them clearly.

He begged Pettr to speak to him, and suddenly, Lupé knew there were four words to the mantra of the birds of pray, four words that would unlock the mysteries of Pettr's Earth. And Lupé already knew one of these words. More than that, he knew that something had heard his prayers—the wind, the sea . . . possibly Pettr himself.

Lupé felt dizzy, as if he were tumbling out of control in a violent headwind. He tried to resist, but a gusty breath deep within told him not to fight the gale, to tumble with it. The unfamiliar voice instructed Lupé to steady himself and allow the wind to carry him where it would. It was the wind speaking to Lupé: Pettr's wind.

The petrel understood the instructions and surrendered to the vision. His awareness soared into a flock of clouds that hovered high above a small group of islands. The petrel drifted through cool, crisp air that had never touched the inside of a lung before. He savored every second of the revelation.

Below, eighteen tiny islands dotted the sea, an isolated archipelago. He believed he might have seen these islands before. He was sure they were real.

When the wind spoke again, Lupé heard, "Do not accept the terms of the man-flock. Ready yourself, and you will be carried to the Islands of Life. Remember what they look like. This is the kingdom where you will . . ."

The wind disappeared, and the message went with it. Lupé awoke in the silver web, dizzy and scared. Gone was the vision of his prayers. Now shining in his mind's eye was the image of the old butterfly sitting on the robins' egg, still grinning at him. The petrel was confused.

As the image slowly faded, Lupé's attention was drawn to the flowers sitting atop the noisy light in the burrow. Lupé noticed that two petals had fallen from the flowers. When they refused to settle on the ground, he realized that they were attached. They were moving together in a synchronized, fluttering rhythm, coming toward him. It looked like a flying flower of bright orange and black touched with wisps of white. As it drew closer, the petrel couldn't believe what he saw. It was the butterfly that approached, his slippery friend from the nest outside.

Lupé wondered, *How did he get in here . . . and why would he want to?*

The butterfly flew nearer. Lupé noticed that his path would bring him very close to a strange, dangerous man-flock device that glowed an inviting purple, the color of the dragonfly's tail. At times, it made a sharp zapping noise. Other insects had entered the device and never come out. Whatever this thing was, it meant death.

Again, Lupé found himself trying to warn his little friend, and again, the butterfly ignored the warning. Actually, he seemed quite interested in the unique creation that hung in the air. Lupé had heard that butterflies had well developed vision, that they could even see in the ultraviolet spectrum. There was no way the creature could miss the contraption.

Just as the other insects had done, he flew directly at the beguiling glow. Lupé couldn't believe the stupidity of the butterfly as he landed and entered the deadly device. The former egg-sitter paid no attention to the piles of crisp, lifeless insects that surrounded the scary light. The butterfly carefully stepped around their empty bodies, and then he went out of sight. Violent zapping ensued. Lupé cringed with the thought that the butterfly's ancient soul was being burned from his body.

The pale light began to shake and rattle. It zapped louder than it ever had before. It started to swing back and forth. Then it stopped. The butterfly emerged through a veil of fine smoke, a little dizzy, yet unharmed. He smiled at Lupé and prepared to continue his flight toward him. As soon as the butterfly popped into the air, the defeated light plummeted to the ground and smashed into pieces. Lupé was amazed at the luck of this little creature. The quiet visitor landed atop the silver web, looked down at the petrel, and smiled.

There was something about this butterfly that made Lupé feel good inside. He felt unusually calm, relaxed. It was the same feeling he used to get when he was with his mother or grandmother. He had no choice but to return the creature's infectious smile. "Just my luck," the petrel mused. "You float in here for the fun of it, and I'd do anything to be able to get out."

Lupé had seen plenty of butterflies before, and he knew there were two things butterflies never did. They never spoke. Perhaps it was because they didn't have mouths, Lupé guessed. And they never listened to anything anyone told them. So Lupé usually didn't pay too much attention to them either, but this butterfly seemed to demand attention.

Not at all satisfied with his perch on top of the silver web, the insect started to climb down the side. Lupé was impressed with the agility of the aged butterfly. Watching his colorful friend lower himself all the way to the base of the web, Lupé wondered why he didn't just fly.

But before Lupé could find an answer to his question, the butterfly pulled his wings together above his body and strolled through a slit into the petrel's space, flashing that huge grin the entire time. The two creatures stood face to face and just stared at each other, the butterfly dwarfed by the size of the bird.

Lupé gazed into the jet-black eyes that radiated with the brilliance of comprehension. The spark of knowledge burned inside the little body, so much so that it surged through its shimmering eyes. It was the touch of those sparks, those little beams of life, that made Lupé feel so calm, so safe.

The petrel had a feeling that there was a great deal of power behind those tiny black peepers. As old as the butterfly seemed to be on the outside, those eyes suggested that a curious—perhaps mischievous—youth lived within. Left alone, it was obvious the insect would enjoy many more years of egg-sitting and zapper fighting.

Next, Lupé couldn't help but marvel at the fragile wings. He was confused as to why a creature with such splendid wings would need six legs and feet. But it was really the wings that made them brothers. He began to lose himself in the intricate patterns of orange, black, and white. The petrel knew that these wings, thinner than a single sheet of dried seaweed, held special power: the incredible power of flight. He wondered when he would use his own power again.

"Very soon," Lupé heard from within the web. He nearly fell over with surprise.

He stared directly at the butterfly, lowered his head so they could be face to face, and asked, "Did you say something?"

The butterfly smiled.

Lupé continued, "Do not fool with me. I am a desperate bird. I ask you again, did you speak to me?"

The grin disappeared, and the old butterfly slowly shifted his antennae. Lupé had never heard one speak before. He waited to hear what the insect would tell him, what wisdom he would impart. The proboscis, a built-in straw used to sip nectar and other liquids, uncoiled completely, and then the butterfly . . . yawned. He turned, retracted his proboscis, and walked out of the silver web, where the petrel could not follow.

Letting his frustration get the better of him, Lupé yelled, "Do not try to come back in here, dried-up old petal . . . unless you wish to see the inside of my belly!" But Lupé would not eat the butterfly, and the butterfly surely knew that. It was a Monarch, and it was filled with a toxin that would make the petrel quite ill, a wonderful trait that allowed the insect to be bold beyond his appearance.

As soon as the words left his beak, Lupé felt foolish for having said them. He knew butterflies couldn't speak, and he felt bad for chasing the old smiler away. He also had the feeling that it would not be so easy to make a meal out of this butterfly, regardless of the bitter taste it might leave.

That night, Lupé was again visited by Zomis, who made fast work of all the petrel's leftovers while Lupé tried to tell his friend about the butterfly. Zomis did not listen. The rat-bird had only one thing on its small mind: food.

Even after many nights together, Lupé was still amazed at how much Zomis physically resembled a rat. Its posture, habits, look, and smell all declared "rodent." Even the pigeon's coo had morphed into a rat-like snivel.

Zomis's feathers, which were once fluffy and light, were now matted so flat with oil and dirt, they looked more like bristly hairs than feathers for flight. Lupé was sure Zomis was far too heavy to fly anymore, and those dirty, unpracticed wings could be good for only one thing: hoarding scraps for their hungry host. It was a point Zomis was all too happy to prove.

Lupé found himself asking, "Zomis, how can you eat like this? Don't you miss flying, gathering, the whole experience of feeding? Your body never leaves the ground, and you live on the scraps of others. How can . . ."

Zomis looked up from the other side of the silver web. The pigeon was so upset, it actually stopped chewing, then gathered its girth and slowly waddled toward Lupé. Only the hard silver web stood between them. When the angry rat-bird laid its bulk against it, the entire structure rattled.

Zomis spoke quietly but forcefully. "I am what you see. I live this way because I choose to. Who are you to say what is better? Yes, I am free to fly and eat worms and seeds, but I am also free not to fly, not to eat worms and seeds if I choose."

Lupé carefully interrupted. He did not want to anger the large Zomis any further. "But what of the wonderful experience of gathering your meal, the ritual your kind has performed since the beginning? You love to eat sooo much, surely you are above scavenging."

A look came over Zomis that Lupé had not seen since the first time they met, when Lupé sprayed the pigeon with hot oil. Zomis was obviously hurt and disappointed by the petrel's criticism.

Shaking its tiny head, Zomis replied, "What is *above* and what is *below*? Who decides what is better, what is worse? Or what is right, what is wrong? I will decide for me . . . And when was the last time you flew for your food?"

Lupé shot back, "Had I the opportunity, I would. But I have no choice. You do."

"And I have chosen," Zomis countered. "Why is scavenging not as wonderful as anything else? I live for the moment every night when I emerge from my hole and scurry from web to web, seeing what lovely morsels wait for me. It's all I want. I kill nothing. I waste nothing. Why would I take something else from this world when this has already been taken? Why isn't my harmony with the Earth every bit as beautiful as yours?"

Zomis turned away, drained and tired.

Lupé never suspected that the pigeon could be so serious and make so much sense. Zomis was the strangest bird he had ever met, but they were friends, and Lupé realized he had hurt Zomis deeply. For the second time in one day, Lupé felt empty. He had chased away the only two friends he had had in a very long time, friends who had actually come to see him.

Now the petrel understood that there were two reasons why Zomis liked him so much. First and foremost, Lupé had terrific food to share. But almost as important, Zomis must have felt drawn to Lupé because the petrel always accepted whoever, whatever the pigeon—the rat—decided to do with its life. Any judgment had been based solely on character. Lupé knew he had violated that trust.

The petrel squeezed his beak through the silver web and gingerly poked Zomis's flab several times. The messy mass began to jiggle and bounce. After a third poke, Zomis began to sniggle a giggle. Then the rat-bird's crazier side re-emerged as Zomis tumbled against the web, laughing. Lupé smiled in anticipation, waiting to be let in on the joke, but Zomis did not stop laughing until Lupé grabbed that rat-bird's greasy tail-feathers with his beak and tried pulling one out.

When Lupé tugged, neither Zomis nor the tail-feathers budged. The petrel, however, was pulled clean off his feet and crashed into the web himself. After seeing this, Zomis stopped chuckling and instead screeched with laughter. It was the one thing Zomis had to do like a bird, because rats never actually laugh. They only sneer, or snicker on occasion.

Finally, Lupé demanded, "So you find me falling that funny?"

"Oh, yes! But it's not . . . coo hoo hoo . . . not, coo hooo, just you," the rat-bird choked.

"What else could it possibly be?" Lupé cawed as he regained his feet and brushed his feathers off.

"It's just the idea . . . the notion of me flying like a bird and eating worms and seeds . . . worms and seeds! Coo hoo hoo. Oh, it's just too funny," Zomis said while sucking up an unattended morsel.

At this point, Lupé was happy his friend was somewhat hairbrained. He was happy Zomis could turn pain into laughter and wished he could do the same with the pain of his captivity.

Then Zomis cut in. "Coo hoo hoo . . . don't . . . hoo hoo . . . think I've forgotten, coo hoo. You still hurt my feelings before."

Lupé's disappointment with himself returned. The pigeon's head was not quite so mixed up after all.

Zomis regained himself and continued, "So now you have to give me something special . . . something very special that I can eat. And we'll be friends again."

Lupé smiled. This was the Zomis he knew and loved. He also knew just what to do. The petrel turned, looked down, and poked through some scraps of food with his beak. He extended his wing to brush away some squid and some shrimp. Then he found it, a small clam that the man-flock had not opened for him. And even though he couldn't eat it like this, the unopened clam made Lupé feel happy. It was the closest he would come to feeding himself. The clam reminded him of his freedom.

It was a tight squeeze, but Lupé managed to push the clam through the silver web to Zomis, who waited with anticipation. Once it was through, Zomis pecked at the hard shell until it was dizzy. Lupé told him to wait, but Zomis was too absorbed with the potential meal to pay any attention to the petrel. When the ravenous rat-bird had pecked itself silly, it finally seemed to understand that the shell was harder than its beak.

Lupé asked, "Are you through?"

Zomis looked up suspiciously, wondering if the clam was some sort of trick, a ploy meant to embarrass.

Now that Lupé had Zomis's attention, he instructed his friend to push the clam over the ledge where the silver web sat and then to bring the clam back up to him after it struck the shiny, hard ground below.

Zomis did as instructed. The pigeon shoved the clam over the edge. There was a loud *crack*. Lupé's friend disappeared and then reappeared, out of breath, dragging the prize. The petrel had never seen his chubby companion move so fast.

Zomis said, "Why did you tell me to do that? Look, the shell is broken."

"And it's lucky for you it is," Lupé quipped.

The clam was cracked in several places. Lupé picked the shell apart with his beak, which was longer, stronger, and more practiced at this chore than his friend's. Together, he and Zomis shared the bounty of the clam. It was the most enjoyable meal Lupé had had since his capture. For Zomis, the clam was one of the most enjoyable meals it had had that evening.

Things went on much the same between Lupé and Zomis. They met every night and talked while they ate. Needless to say, most of the eating and talking was done by Zomis. Lupé was still miserable at being kept, and he constantly worried about how he could save his flock, but having a friend made it all a little easier to cope with. He thanked Pettr for sending Zomis to him. He wondered what his God's purpose was.

Would Zomis figure into his escape from the man-flock, or would the rat-bird be the last friend he'd ever know?

One rainy night while the two friends sat together, the silver web still between them, the wind started to call Lupé again. Gradually, the clear night sky grew darker. The bright stars faded from sight, shrouded behind a dense bank of clouds. The wind joined in, swirling and whistling with mischief. The elements were combining forces. It was something Lupé had learned to fear, because it usually spelled "storm."

The petrel grew quiet, yet restless. He made no noise, but he stretched his wings nervously. Flapping them with great force, he lifted himself off the ground until his head bumped against the top of the web that contained him. He did this over and over. Zomis tried to calm the bird, but Lupé did not respond. He felt distant, removed. The petrel wanted the wind, and it appeared the wind wanted him. That night, it was Lupé who appeared crazy. This scared Zomis. The rat-bird backed away into the safety of the shadows, waiting for Lupé to regain his senses.

As the branch outside tapped against the opening, the petrel began to respond to the sound it made. The louder the tap, the wilder he became. Thunder cracked and snapped outside. It looked to Zomis like Lupé and the storm were connected somehow. Each grew more intense with the other.

Just as the petrel reached the point where it seemed he might seriously hurt himself, he became quiet and still. He had sensed a presence. With glazed eyes, he scanned the web, convinced that something had joined him inside. He wasn't sure what it was. He wondered if the wind was coming to free him, or maybe it was Pettr himself. He couldn't tell if this presence was something to be feared. Then he saw what had joined him. The old butterfly had returned.

He strolled around Lupé's space as if it were his own, paying no attention to the storm that raged outside. The calm of the silent visitor contrasted greatly with the violence of the weather. As Lupé watched the butterfly, he became transfixed, frozen. He couldn't twitch a feather.

Zomis started to worry about Lupé. He wanted the petrel to snap out of the trance, so the rat-bird decided to chase the butterfly away.

Like he had read the pigeon's thoughts, Lupé turned toward the black shadows and whispered, "He's here to help me . . . I think."

The butterfly fluttered away and landed on the sealed opening that separated the storm from Lupé. When he looked back at the petrel, the huge beaming grin reappeared.

Lupé could not pry his eyes from the portal. He and the old butterfly watched the clouds roll as an occasional crisp of lightning creased the sky. The petrel's gaze became a glare. Lupé became hypnotized by the way the wind jarred the limbs of the tree outside. They shook back and forth while they tapped at the opening, calling Lupé to it. Moved by the wind, the tree seemed to dance for Lupé. It soothed him, just like the smile of the butterfly, but on another level, there was something unsettling about both.

The storm continued to rage, and the erratic tapping of the branch grew louder, stronger. Then the robin's nest that clung to the throbbing limb snapped free and slid toward the sealed opening.

Suddenly, the old butterfly popped into the air, just as the branch broke from the tree and exploded through the opening, shattering it and letting the robin's nest drop in. The silver web rattled as debris rained in. It shook violently while the wind, the rain, and the night all surged into the room. Spinning and whistling, the wind found Lupé. The breath of the planet had come to him.

Gone was the glazed look. Now the petrel's heart beat wildly. He was wide awake. He knew that Pettr had answered his prayers by sending the wind and the butterfly to free him. But Lupé was still inside the silver web, and he had no idea how to get out. Above the cracking of the thunder and the howling of the wind, Lupé heard rocking, a quiet creaking from within the web.

He turned slowly and saw the butterfly next to him swaying back and forth on a broken shard of clam shell.

The happy insect smiled his smile and bobbed his head to the rhythm of the shell, back and forth, back and forth.

At first, Lupé thought the old butterfly was as crazy as Zomis. This was no time to be rocking merrily. Then the petrel understood that the butterfly was trying to tell him something. He watched and concentrated. The shell gleamed and sparkled as it rose and fell. Lupé knew what he had to do.

He beckoned his plump friend to emerge from the shadows. "Zomis!" The word had barely crossed Lupé's beak when his companion appeared at his side. "Shove the web over the edge!" Lupé cawed.

Zomis looked confused and said, "But if I do that, you'll be hurt . . . I can't. I won't. You're not yourself tonight. You don't know what you're saying."

Lupé had to think fast. An opportunity might be slipping away. "Shove me over the edge, you fat, feathered, egg-laying pigeon."

Zomis looked hard at Lupé.

"Come on, you cooing seed-eater," the petrel taunted.

The rat-bird's expression became fierce as it gathered its bulk. "Shove me over the ledge, you . . . *bird!*"

That was all it would take. Zomis's body began to swell. The pigeon lowered its head and charged Lupé with all of its might. Zomis wanted to run through the mesh and pounce on the antagonizer—crush the life out of him if possible.

Lupé knew what was coming and braced himself against the far side of the web.

When the rat-bird threw itself at Lupé, both the petrel and the silver web were launched over the ledge. They hit the ground with a crash and a tumble.

The butterfly, who seemed to be enjoying all of this, was flitting about overhead when Lupé noticed the web had broken open, just like the clam he had shared with Zomis.

He struggled through the crack, and for the first time since his capture, he was free to go.

Lupé cawed loudly and looked toward the opening. He was ready to join the wind in the clouds. As he stretched his wings and prepared to fly . . . he was slammed to the floor under the considerable weight of Zomis.

"Now you'll answer to a rat!" Zomis hissed. "And what I leave of you will not be worth scavenging by another."

The petrel tried to wriggle out from under his attacker, but he could not. Frantically, he moved his head from side to side to avoid the thrusts of Zomis's small, sharp beak. Finally, Lupé blew a thick stream of hot orange oil over Zomis and down the rat-bird's open beak.

Zomis gagged and rolled off Lupé.

Immediately, the petrel flapped into the air toward the opening. After a second, he stopped himself and circled back to check on his pigeon friend. He perched next to Zomis and said, "Forgive me, my friend. But I needed you to push me over the edge. I'm sorry I had to do the same to you. There was no meaning behind the words I used. Now I have to leave. I will never forget you."

"No meaning?" Zomis asked.

"None."

"I will miss you too." The rat-bird grinned as it continued, "There's only one thing I will miss more than your company . . . and that's your lovely leftovers."

Lupé laughed and brushed his wing against Zomis. It was the first time he had freely touched his friend, and he was reminded that there was no longer a web between them. A strange thought occurred to the petrel. He remembered that he had never been able to say goodbye to his friends on Gwatta when the man-flock had captured him. Lupé pushed the thought aside. Now was not the time.

Zomis looked Lupé in the eye. For a moment, the chubby bird seemed completely normal, a proud example of "pigeondom." It tilted its head slightly to one side, looked to the opening, and nodded. Then it said, "May the wind be at your back." It was the ancient farewell that bound all birds as brothers and sisters. The words filled Lupé with power and purpose.

In an instant, there was bright light everywhere. One of the man-flock had entered and was looking directly at Lupé and Zomis. The intruder waved a long branch with a thick nest of dried grass bound to the end of it while he positioned himself between the two birds and the bare opening. He stepped toward the pair, sweeping down with the stick to scatter the birds in opposite directions.

Zomis screamed, "Fly, Lupé! Fly!"

The intruder seemed to be more interested in Lupé than Zomis, and he pursued the petrel. He swung the stick at Lupé, trying to sweep him into a corner. The petrel was so busy dodging the stick, he could not gather himself to fly.

It looked like Lupé would be returned to the silver web until Zomis decided to get involved. Prepared to do whatever it took to protect the petrel, Zomis charged the attacker, running as fast as its little legs would carry the large body. While Zomis gathered speed and momentum, it extended its forgotten wings. They were dirty, twisted things that hadn't been used for many years, yet Zomis seemed to remember the meaning of their existence. And as the pigeon flapped and shook the dirt from them, its great bulk lifted off the ground.

Working furiously, the plump rat-bird managed to raise itself a few feet in the air. The wings pumped harder and harder, and the pigeon picked up speed. Lupé watched in amazement while Zomis propelled its robust body at the only thing that stood between the petrel and freedom.

The one from the man-flock turned and faced Zomis.

Dodging a swipe of the stick at the last second, the flying rat-bird lowered its head and struck with full force in the region where the intruder's legs met his torso.

Zomis must have been flying faster than it appeared, because the creature screamed, stumbled, and fell backward. But as the one from the man-flock tumbled, he reached out with the stick and smashed Zomis to the ground.

Lupé flew to his friend.

Before the petrel could speak, Zomis stood, somewhat wobbly, and said, "Quick, before he rises again, fly!"

"Thank you!" Lupé replied. He leapt into the air and added, "One day, a petrel from my flock will bear your name!"

Lupé raced toward the opening.

As he did so, the long stick with the nest returned to life. The one from the man-flock rose. He reared back to swat the escaping petrel from the air. Suddenly, he froze on his feet.

This time, it was the old butterfly who flew to Lupé's rescue. The tiny creature soared with incredible speed right at the head of the one with the stick. He landed on the intruder's nose and spread his wings over the creature's eyes.

The intruder jumped up and down, shaking his head from side to side, refusing to release his grasp on the dangerous stick, but the crusty old butterfly held on. The stick flew in every direction yet never once came close to Lupé, who passed through the opening unscathed.

As the one from the man-flock grew more desperate and enraged, he swung the stick directly at his own head, hoping to crush the fragile butterfly who clung to his face.

Just when it seemed certain the intruder would accomplish his horrible purpose, the old butterfly twittered away, and the stick broke across the intruder's nose.

This time, when the one from the man-flock hit the ground, he did not move until well after sunrise. The pounding in his head and the sharp pain that lingered between his legs served as a potent reminder of the power of lesser creatures.

It seemed as though the moment Lupé flew through the window, the storm disappeared. The sky became clear, the wind dropped to a whisper, and the air tasted sweet. Lupé landed on what was left of the tree outside to collect himself. He was free, but he wasn't exactly sure what to do next. It had all happened so fast.

The petrel closed his eyes for a moment. When he opened them, he found his favorite butterfly standing at his side, smiling. The wind tugged at his feathers, and Lupé knew where he would have to go. Whether he got there or not was quite another issue.

The petrel turned to the butterfly and said, "I doubt I'll ever see you again, my brave friend. Tonight, because of you and Zomis, I have my freedom. And tonight, I must leave you both forev-

er. Thank you for delivering me from the man-flock, for giving me the chance to save my flock. My search begins."

Lupé looked back through the opening for the last time. What he saw surprised him and brought a smile to his beak. He and the butterfly shared a wide grin as they watched what was happening inside.

Zomis, now standing again, had found something interesting.

Lupé chuckled as he saw his robust friend dragging the robin's nest, graced with a recently hatched chick that had somehow survived the crash, toward the hole in the wall. The nest fit easily through the hole, although it was still a tight squeeze for Zomis. Lupé could see that those greasy feathers did serve a purpose when Zomis's extremities barely slipped through the crack.

The rat-bird would become a parent. It was an irony that warmed Lupé.

The petrel climbed into the cool night sky, wondering whether the chick would be raised as bird or rodent. But he knew the answer really didn't matter, because the chick would be Zomis's child, and that was enough.

Part Two

Weathering the Storm

With nothing but a wing and a prayer, Lupé burst into the dawn sky. A pink sunrise hailed the beginning of his migration to the Islands of Life. Although he was still many miles inland, Lupé could smell the sea. Instinctively, he pursued the vast waters.

Looking down from his flight, Lupé saw many trees, hills, and small streams. But more than anything else, the planet was covered with the immense nests of the man-flock. Trees were cut, hills were flattened, fields were cleared, and streams were drained, all to make room for the countless nests and the wide, hard paths that scarred the planet's skin.

Some of the nests were so tall, they reached up into the clouds, higher than the highest trees, never noticing the little petrel chasing the sea. Lupé gazed at the massive structures created by the man-flock, and a sad smile crossed his beak. He was reminded of something Kurah had told him as a chick.

His father had just been putting the finishing touches on a fresh nest, a nest any petrel would be proud to call its own. Although most from his flock chose to burrow into the dirt and sand, Kurah had felt a nest could be safer. He liked to be able to see what approached without being cornered underground.

Lupé recalled the help he had given his father, how he had gathered all the loose twigs and debris he could find and carried them to the site, a shaded ridge not far from shore, covered with dwarf pines and shy oaks, protected by a rocky outcrop. When

Kurah finished, a snug nest sat softly among the rocks. The mature petrel nodded approvingly, smiled to his son, and then flew off to feed.

The more Lupé examined the nest, the more he became convinced he could improve it. So while Kurah was away, Lupé began his alterations. By the time his father returned, the young petrel had piled enough twigs around the original nest to house several families. The cozy creation of Kurah was now a massive, sloppy pile of debris.

As usual, Father said nothing. He looked over his son's work, and then he looked a little longer. While Lupé waited to be congratulated on his craftsbirdship and sense of style, Kurah hopped over to the mound and began removing excess twigs. Somewhere under there, he hoped, his original nest survived.

This was too much for Lupé. He screeched, "Father, what are you doing? I helped you make the greatest nest on the island! None is bigger than ours! We are living large!"

Kurah dropped the twigs from his strong beak and turned to his son. "I thank you for your help, Lupé, but what makes a nest great is not its size. The only thing that can glorify any home are the birds who live in it. Their nest will only be as special as they are."

Father leaned over and slowly ran his beak up and down the little one's neck. He whispered to Lupé, "Always fly the good flight. Only your spirit will bring honor to this spot, not a bunch of twigs."

As is often the case with small birds, Lupé only partially understood what his father was saying, but happy for the chance to help, he joined Kurah in removing the excess. When they were almost done, Lupé made one last appeal.

"But look how big, how soft I made it," the little one peeped.

"You are right, son," Kurah replied. "It is big, and it is soft, but does that make it better?"

Now Lupé was really confused. He looked at his father, smiled, and nodded his head.

So Kurah asked, "On cold nights, what keeps you warm?"

Lupé thought carefully. "You and Mother covering me."

"In a nest this size, would you stay warm?"

Lupé began to understand.

"On dark nights, when the snake is hungry, what keeps him from my sleeping son?" Kurah continued.

Again, Lupé thought. "The snake must pass you and Mother before he can reach me!"

"When the hungry hawk flies overhead, who is he looking for to become his meal?"

"Little ones." Then Lupé swallowed hard and added, "Like me."

"So, my son, what size nest keeps you warmer, safer, and hides you from the hawk in the clouds?"

"The little one!" Lupé laughed.

Kurah nodded, and together, they removed the rest of the twigs.

Later that evening, when Lupé, Kurah, and Raza were nestling down for the night, Lupé, never one to give up on a new thought or idea, popped his head up between his parents and asked, "Okay, I know it's better to have a small nest. So if I can make one too big, can I also make one too small? How will I ever know what size is just right?"

Raza looked down and answered her son's question with another question. "From where you sleep, little one, what do you see?"

Lupé looked all around him, concentrated, and screeched, "Two large rumps!"

"Good!" Raza cackled. She continued sincerely, but slightly ruffled by the realization that her rump could seem that large to someone. "Now you know how big your nest should be . . . large enough for two adult rumps. The young will squeeze in between."

The last thing Lupé remembered hearing that night before he fell asleep was his mother whispering to his father, "Does my rump really seem that—" And then the petrel had nodded off.

Although this was a very happy memory, Lupé was saddened by the thought that his next nest would probably be a lonely one, only one-third full.

Whenever he was faced with a long flight, Lupé liked to look back at his younger days. It helped him feel as though his family was still with him, and in one sense, maybe they were.

Pressing on toward the sea, Lupé was amazed at how many nests the man-flock had built. He had learned long ago to avoid the glow of the tiny suns of the man-flock. Their light meant danger, but since the petrel was already surrounded by them and there seemed to be no getting away from this glow, Lupé ignored the dead light and continued to fly to the ocean.

The petrel's thoughts returned to the man-flock and how they seemed blind to the beauty of Pettr's Earth. He wondered why anyone would want to destroy something so perfect. Lupé decided that the man-flock probably didn't see the beauty, and that was what enabled them to act the way they did. He felt sad for them.

As the sun rose higher in the sky, Lupé looked forward to seeing the many colors of life that would splash across the planet. He had waited a long time for this opportunity. Magnificent in its own right, the sky usually offered blues and whites, but the Earth presented greens, golds, reds, browns—every color, shade, and blend imaginable. This was especially exciting to the pelagic petrel. All these colors were alive, all part of Pettr's plan. Lupé became more eager to see it as he pictured the scene in his mind.

When the sun burned away the morning clouds, Lupé saw that the once-vibrant colors had faded. The planet actually looked sick. The trees that had covered the Earth like feathers on a bird were gone. *The man-flock clipped the wings of the planet*, Lupé thought, *just as they clipped my wings.* He considered who would perish first, his flock or the planet. The once-healthy Earth, especially in this area, was now covered with unnatural cuts, scabs, and blisters—all evidence of the disease spreading below. Depressed but determined, the petrel flew on.

Before he saw it, before he could taste it, Lupé heard it: the roar, the thunder, the spill of the ocean slamming the shore. It was constant, wonderful. And then the smell became thick. At first, wet wisps of salt were carried to the clouds. As the sound of surf grew louder and clearer, the salty air became more dense. Lupé pumped furiously, drinking it all in. It was what he had waited so long for. Then he saw it—the sea. For the first time since he was tangled in a net and grabbed by a hand, the petrel felt truly free.

Without thinking, he climbed higher in the sky until he was up among the thin clouds, where he flew lazy circles while the sweet sea waited below. Lupé wept as he thanked Pettr. Then he folded his wings to his sides and dove at the blue-blue ocean.

Lupé sliced through the clouds and emerged with dew dripping from his beak. Plummeting to the stirring sea, his feathers fell flat against his body. The petrel dove with such speed, he thought the plumage might be pulled from his face. Below, there was nothing but ocean, deep and vast. Lupé was finally surrounded by his two favorite colors, the rich blue of the ocean met by the gentle blue of a clear sky.

The petrel thought, *This is what it must be like to pass through Pettr's eye and live on the other side with the Lord.* It was then that he landed on the more quiet, deep water with a tiny splash. Bobbing up and down on soft, rolling swells, he thanked Pettr again.

As Lupé flew further out to sea, the only sound that joined the wind and the ocean was the *thup-thup-thup* of his liberated wings. The sound was so soothing, so missed, the petrel welled with emotion. Like a chick hearing its mother's heartbeat through her feathered breast, he felt secure, reborn.

Lupé flew under the sun as it started to fall away from the Smaller Sea. He watched the wind blow a peaceful shadow across the cool water. The Gwatta was immersed in the rich blue of day.

Although he wasn't exactly sure where the Islands of Life were, Lupé did have a strong feeling as to where he should search. Now that Pettr's eye was closing, Lupé would turn so that the leg that bore the silver band of the man-flock would be alongside the sun. He would fly in that direction, down toward warmer water, straight through the night. If all went well and the wind cooperated with Zomis's farewell, the eye of Pettr would rise in the morning on the side opposite the silver band.

Once Lupé was well into temperate water, it would be time to change course. He would fly away from the rising sun, into the setting sun until he reached the sea of his birth, the Ocean of Peace. He believed that somewhere in that great body of water, the Islands of Life waited for him. Lupé hoped that sometime during his journey, Pettr would provide him with a hint as to the exact location of the islands. Even without the clue, Lupé trusted that sooner or later, Pettr's wind would blow the way.

The petrel had flown for quite some time and was well into his journey when his breast began to ache. The wing he had twice injured at the hands of the man-flock began to throb and burn. Lupé was puzzled by the pain, because he knew he had not flown long enough to feel like this. There would certainly be pain by the end of his journey, but not yet.

Then Lupé understood. He was out of shape. His once awesome power of flight had deteriorated. For the first time in his life, the anxious petrel wondered whether he was physically capable of reaching his destination. He gathered muscle and will, clenched his beak, and flew toward the answer.

Lupé told himself, *If I am going to be beaten, I will not beat myself. Something else must defeat me.*

Unsure of what lay ahead, Lupé decided to count his blessings and concentrate on the positive. Pettr had been good to him. His savior had heard his prayers and provided Zomis, the butterfly, and the wind. Lupé reasoned that Pettr would not have helped him escape only to let him die later searching for the islands. The petrel believed that as long as he kept his faith, Pettr would provide.

As he flew on, Lupé became deaf to the pounding of the little heart straining within him. Instead, he let the sound of the water below intoxicate him. It was the sound he dreamt of and lived for. It was a sound that nourished him. Gazing down at the sea, Lupé started to feel better. The water below was cool and clean. It rippled quietly and glistened beneath a watchful, warming sun.

Clean water always pleased the petrel. It meant the sea was healthy and full of life. But too often, that was not the case. Lupé had seen the black death before. He knew firstwing what it was like to feel the heavy muck cling to his feathers. He had witnessed the black sludge kill those above the sea and those below the sea.

He wasn't sure where it came from, but he guessed that something hurt the sea and the deadly black oozed to the surface, as if the planet itself was wounded and bleeding. But what Lupé didn't understand was why this muck killed the birds and the fish. Why did it kill those who loved the sea the most?

He wondered if the deadly slime was a warning from Pettr. Lupé imagined the Creator saying, "Those who pretend to love the sea should protect the sea. If you allow it to become barren, it is you who will become barren. So goes the sea, so goes you." The petrel believed this was the message behind the black death, but he did not know what he should protect the ocean from or how to do it. Maybe Pettr would tell him.

For now, there was no black death floating on the ocean. Lupé was encouraged. He hoped the sea had stopped bleeding, that Pettr had realized the birds were not to blame, and that whatever caused the ocean's pain had gone away.

For some strange reason, Lupé's thoughts glided to "dirt." And then from there, his ruminations landed on Zomis. Was the rat-bird teaching its chick to flap its wings or to snivel and scurry in search of scraps? Knowing Zomis as he did, the petrel envisioned the pigeon stuffing the hole in the wall with a mountain of tasty morsels, eating until all parent and chick could do was lie there, smile at each other, and peep an occasional burp.

It had almost slipped Lupé's mind, but thinking about his portly friend made him realize something—he was hungry. Lupé guessed that his hunger might be one of the reasons for his chest pains. He wasn't really sure, because he hadn't felt hunger pains for quite some time. The petrel had always eaten well when he was free. And if the man-flock did anything, they provided plenty of food. Now that Lupé was free again, it was time for him to feed himself. He looked forward to performing the ritual.

However, Lupé was now flying over a different ocean. This was the Smaller Ocean, a huge body of water, but not his home, the larger Ocean of Peace. Judging from the problems he was having with flying, Lupé worried that his fishing skills might also need work. But it was time to feed, so Lupé laughed off his concerns and began to search for the little fishes in the deep green below. He was so anxious to feed that his beak dripped and his belly bellowed as he scanned the rolling water.

After what felt like a migration, Lupé spotted a welcome sight. A shoal of anchovies popped through the surface. He took a deep breath and smiled to himself. This was what he had waited for, what he had envisioned while he was held. Lupé hovered above the swimming fish and prepared to gather his meal. Then he dove.

As Lupé approached the surface of the sea, he slowed, skimmed his beak across the water, and was immediately rewarded with sustenance. It tasted just as he remembered. The petrel swallowed the fish whole and prepared for another pass. When he was ready to dive again, Lupé realized he had a problem. The little fish had disappeared deep below the sea.

Lupé glided, floated, and waited. Then they reappeared. Lupé flew to them, skimmed out a single anchovy, swallowed it, and realized the school was gone again.

The petrel decided to employ a different strategy. He would hover only a few inches above the sea. When the little fish surfaced, Lupé would be closer to them and might be able to catch a few more before they moved away.

While Lupé waited with his beak poised, he felt an itch under his wing. Well, any hatchling knows that it's almost impossible to fly and scratch at the same time, but without thinking, Lupé stretched his beak under his wing and scratched at the source of irritation. Immediately, he felt better, and immediately, he plummeted into the sea.

Completely caught by surprise, Lupé shook the water from his feathers while he floated on the ocean. Never before had this happened to him. Never before had he been "dipped," as the petrels called it. Only the most awkward, clumsy adolescents allowed themselves to be dipped. Lupé was thoroughly embarrassed.

Shaking water from the oily feathers on his head, the petrel caught himself searching the sky to see if any other birds had witnessed his complete incompetence. He realized he was alone on the sea, and now he was glad of it. It made it easier for him to laugh at his foolishness.

It dawned on Lupé that he had another problem. Migration required a lot of food, and Lupé, besides being out of shape, had not eaten nearly enough before he had escaped the man-flock to prepare for such a journey. Following Zomis's example might not have been such a bad idea.

Eating one or two small fish would certainly not sustain him, especially if he had to work hard to conquer wind or weather. Getting dipped only proved to him that his feeding skills were not what they once had been.

Even at their sharpest, petrels were not meant to feed alone. It usually took several birds to spot and track schools of fish. Alone, with rusty skills on an unfamiliar ocean, Lupé was in trouble. He had to fly to feed himself and to get home, but the more he flew, the hungrier he would get.

Lupé stopped his panic from going any further. He reminded himself that he was free. Succeed or perish, it was all that mattered. It was the only truth. He swore that he would not dwell on the obstacles. Everything would be fine; he was a very lucky bird. So he thanked Pettr for the modest meal and continued his trek.

No matter what he swore to himself, subconsciously, Lupé still tried to find a way to feed. The longer he flew, the emptier his belly felt. He had no idea whether the pain that pulsed through his body stemmed from hunger, a strained heart, or from wings too long contained in the silver web. Perhaps it was all three.

By the end of his third consecutive day of flight, Lupé gave serious consideration to whether he should head toward shore to rest. It was something he hoped he could avoid. It would mean delay and danger. On Peace, he knew every island, atoll, and predator, but the Smaller Ocean was unfamiliar. As his wings pushed forward, reaching for more sky, Lupé had the feeling it was time to pray.

He closed his eyes and climbed high into the blue, allowing the wind to steer for him. Surrounded by nothing but sky, the struggling bird called to Pettr. He asked for a sign. Should he press on, or should he take the risk and rest?

The wind remained silent, and Lupé heard no voice from within. He stayed high in the clouds and flapped blindly on, waiting for an answer. His injured wing began to drag against the cool air, but Lupé pressed on, meditating as he flew.

It slowly dawned on the petrel that his course had changed. He believed that the uneven stroke of his weaker wing must have altered his path. Actually, it was the wind that had changed his course. He was being carried somewhere he hadn't planned on going. Then the petrel was reminded of the silver web.

"You will be carried to the Islands of Life," the wind had told him. Was that where he was headed? He was worried, but he had learned long ago from Kurah that it was usually much better to move with the rhythms of the planet than to challenge them. So Lupé continued his awkward stroke, surrendered to the breeze, and hoped for the best.

He had covered a great distance when he spotted something below: a tiny brown speck rising from the shadow of the sea. The wind ceased abruptly, and Lupé tumbled from the current in the sky.

When he finally steadied himself, Lupé noticed that there were other specks in the sea, but they were still very distant and difficult to identify. It looked like the wind had felt his pain and carried him to vast schools of little fish.

Since it seemed the will of the wind, the petrel decided to investigate. Forgetting his aches, and rested from the benevolent breeze, he closed the gap on what he hoped would be a wonderful meal.

As he flew closer, he realized he was approaching a single school of fish, not several. However, one school—even a small one—would still be welcome. But the closer he came, the less likely it seemed this would be a small school. It looked huge . . .

Still closer, his hopes of feasting were dashed when he realized what he pursued was not an enormous school of little fish; rather, it was a little school of enormous fish—whales, actually. For some reason, the wind had carried the starving bird to a pod of giant whales.

Although he was disappointed, Lupé laughed at the thought of trying to skim one of these monsters into his beak. They were now directly beneath him. He hovered a safe distance above the giants and wondered what the wind and Pettr intended. Why was he starved, blown off course, and then delivered to whales? There was nothing here to eat and no other birds to help him fish.

Lupé thought, *As long as I am here, I might as well follow the whales. Pettr must have some reason for all this.*

While the whales flew through the water below, Lupé swam in the sky above. His mind began to drift. The petrel was famished and exhausted. It was difficult to concentrate.

Again, his thoughts returned to his youth, to the islands and to the open sea. He remembered how his father had come home one day with a scratchy old sea gull. Lupé recalled the gull's name was Jopi and that Kurah loved to chat with him. The gull became a frequent visitor to the nest.

If there was one word that described Jopi, it was crusty. He was like a raspy piece of coral that washed up on shore: sharp, salty, and hard. Like coral that breaks free from the reef, Jopi had broken free

from his flock. He was a loner. His friends were few in number but deep in devotion. Perhaps his closest friend was Kurah.

Lupé liked the gull, because Jopi always managed to drop a small fish at Lupé's tiny, webbed feet. The ritual led to an unspoken bond, a special trust between the two birds.

At that time, Lupé was a little too young to eat solid food. Jopi knew this, but he always managed to leave the treat without Kurah or Raza noticing. Although tiny Lupé often choked on the fish and didn't really enjoy the taste, he would never pass up a chance to gobble down Jopi's gift. Eating the same food as the adults made Lupé feel grown up and powerful. He also loved the idea of having a secret from his parents, something only he and the old gull knew about.

Like a flash, it hit him. Lupé knew exactly what Pettr and the wind intended. He remembered the conversation as if it had happened only moments ago. One night, Jopi had told Kurah of an experience he had had on the open sea, over the deep water. The black tide had covered the water where Jopi usually fished. For a long time, there was nothing to eat. When the little fish finally reappeared, those who ate them became sick. Many died.

Jopi decided to leave his flock to search for clean water and safe food. Like Lupé, he was very hungry and thought he might not find a meal in time. He told Kurah he came upon a group of whales. The gull knew that as big as they were, the cetaceans ate the same food as him, just a lot more of it. So he decided to tag along with the whales, who seemed very well fed. When they found their next meal, Jopi would join them . . . carefully.

It wasn't long before the whales came across what they were looking for. As they began to eat, Jopi hovered above the water and picked out the little fish that fled from the mammoth feeders. Jopi followed the giants for several days, eating with them at every opportunity.

When the gull was done with the story, he turned toward the tiny petrel, who hid his head beneath his wing, pretending to be fast asleep, and said, "So you like to hear about the whales? Well, maybe someday, I'll take you to the deep water to feed with them."

Following the whales now as Jopi once did, Lupé wondered if the old gull, who had probably passed through the sun long ago, was somehow managing to keep the promise he had made to a very young petrel.

Suddenly, Lupé was soaked with salt water and slapped high into the sky. He was flying so close to the whales below, he was blasted with spray from a blowhole. Jopi was washed from the petrel's mind as he strained his wet wings to stay aloft. What he saw before him amazed and thrilled him. It was something Jopi had never mentioned in his account of the whales.

The behemoths below formed a wide circle around a dense shoal of the little fish. When the meal was surrounded, the fish raced from one end of the circle to the other. Too frightened to pass through the barrier of whales, they dove below. But a single whale waited beneath the school. He swam a relaxed circle, releasing air bubbles. The bubbles floated up to the surface, extending the impression of a wall under the whales. This made the little fish so confused, they were afraid to pass through the barrier of bubbles. As the whale from below rose to the surface, so did the meal.

Lupé had never seen so many fish gathered in one place at one time. The ocean foamed and churned with panic. Then the whales approached with open mouths. Some ate in one pass what Lupé might eat in a year. The petrel was astounded at how well they worked together to feed each other.

Lupé decided it would be wise to join the feast before the meal disappeared. He knew these hulking mammals would never miss what a starving bird might take. The sea burst with snorting blowholes, gaping jaws, and the slapping of immense tail fins. Occasionally, one of the giants would breach and then slam its bulk against the sea. Even with all the activity, the whales seemed to know Lupé had joined them and took care to allow the petrel to share their feast. Lupé also took care not to get crushed by his new associates.

The petrel hopped nervously atop the water, filling his beak with fleeing fish. It was so easy and Lupé was so hungry, he ate and ate and ate and ate. He didn't know if an opportunity like this would ever come again, so he decided to take full advantage. With one good feeding, the petrel believed he might have enough strength to finish his journey to Peace, so he continued to consume.

Before he knew it, Lupé was straining to swallow, forcing the food down into his full belly. He had ignored the rule that Raza had taught him long ago, a rule that petrels were expected to live by: "Take only what you need, and what you need will always be there to take."

Lupé was still picking out small fish when the whales moved on. *They* knew when they had had enough. Strangely, even after this enormous feeding, the water was still thick with little fish.

The power of great size was matched by the power of great numbers. Both survived, and neither was dangerously diminished. It was Pettr's balance. Now it was time for Lupé to continue his trek, to ensure that the Gwattas would remain part of that balance.

Well after the whales had gone, the little fish dispersed and returned to doing whatever it is the little fish do. Lupé stuffed down a final bite and thanked Pettr for the bounty of the ocean. Then he settled down to float and digest. Lupé laughed when he thought how proud Zomis would have been of his display. He pictured the gluttonous rat-bird drowning itself for the chance to consume such a magnificent meal. He was tickled by the idea that the whales would have turned Zomis away because the pigeon looked capable of eating more than they were.

Amazed that his own bloated belly didn't drag him to the ocean floor, the petrel began to notice something: the sea was getting restless. Maybe the feeding whales were not the only reason the water was so lively before. They were gone now, but the dark sea continued to churn and surge as it gradually grew more intense. The waves were becoming a problem.

Lupé looked up at the sky. The sun was covered. The horizon grew dull and disheartening. Floating on the rollers, the petrel knew a sizeable storm was thundering in. The wind that had purred invitingly a short time ago now breathed heavily. Soon, it might roar.

Lupé was upset with himself. Had he not been in captivity for so long, he would have heard or possibly smelt the storm in plenty of time to avoid it, but his senses were dulled. Only a fool would allow himself to get caught in the deep water at the mercy of a foul wind and an angry sea.

There was also another problem, one that Lupé could only blame himself for. In his present stuffed condition, flight might be very difficult, or worse yet, impossible. The stomach cramps he felt now could not be attributed to hunger; they came from excess.

The *flash-crack* of thunder filled the sky as the storm drew near. It wouldn't be long before the full force of the tempest was upon him. As the rain began to fall, again Lupé wondered why

Pettr would deliver him from the man-flock and starvation only to end his journey unfulfilled on the open sea.

It was time to fly. Lupé used the momentum of a cresting swell to toss himself into flight and knew immediately that he would not be strong enough to lift his bloated body above the torrent. He hoped that the wind would not be nearly as harsh a few feet above the ocean. But even at that low altitude, the wind could still be a gusty, unpredictable problem.

Lupé had trouble orienting himself. Pettr's eye had closed, and the brilliant stars that should have lit the way were hidden behind heavy clouds. The petrel could not decide which direction would put the shearing, turbulent wind predominately at his back. With a little luck, he thought, the storm might actually carry him in the direction he wanted to go. But if what was happening all around him was any indication, Lupé would not be lucky. Realistically, he didn't care how far he was blown off course—he just wanted to survive the storm.

As the foul weather raged on into the night, faint puffs of starlight cut through the pitch sky and feathered the horizon. Lupé was pleased. Like all birds, he knew the stars as well as he knew the

webbing on the top of his feet. Now he might be able to plot some type of course.

The petrel knew that most storms like this flowed up from the warm water. So he fixed his gaze on a familiar star and prepared to fly deeper into the tempest. As Lupé fought on, the weather began to calm. Soon he found himself in the center of the storm. Still far from safe, Lupé believed the worst was over.

He picked up speed and moved easily through the supple air. Rather than rest on the relatively calm sea and wait for the other half of the storm to approach, Lupé hurried through the center. He didn't grasp that he was passing up an opportunity to renew himself as he raced toward trouble.

The wind began to nudge. Lupé lowered himself until he was just a splash from the gray-green ocean. With little resistance he continued to pump along. But as the wind found the ocean, water soaked him. The rain from above and the spray from below made his wings, which were not as well-oiled as they should have been, wet and heavy. And so, flight required even more effort. Knowing he would never be able to lift himself above the turbulence, he did the only thing he could do: he stayed low and pressed on.

Lupé imagined how the sky would clear and the ocean would still once he was through the storm. Then he could rest. When the wind leaned on him, he felt the feathers of his underside skimming across the tops of the swells. With every down stroke, the tips of his wings would dip into the sea. He was wet, heavy, and tired. He was afraid of the darkness and felt as though Pettr was pushing the sky and clouds down on him, forcing him into the sea. Then, just as he tried to lift himself higher into the air, it happened.

The ocean rose up and swallowed him.

For a moment, Lupé thought of the net that had grabbed him long before. But unlike the net, the ocean covered him inside and out. The heavy water that tugged him from the sky filled his tiny lungs and pinned him under the waves. Lupé struggled to stay afloat. He worked wings and webbed feet like never before, paddling, prodding, pushing, pulling, pumping, and finally panicking. The green sea held on, sucking him under.

The bird's beak broke through the churning water, and he cawed a final desperate cry. He became dizzy. He wondered if this was the last time the planet would hear the voice of his flock. Lupé made one more courageous attempt to free himself, to emerge on the wing . . . but again, the sea swallowed him.

It was quiet now. The wind and the ocean were exhausted. There were no wings flapping, no sea birds screeching. Only the calm slap of gentle swells broke the silence. Pettr's opening eye covered the serene sea with fresh sunlight, burning away all traces of the havoc that had raged during the night.

As far as any eye could see, there was nothing but ocean and sky, sky and ocean—one expanse meeting another. But for the keen eye, there was something else, something minute floating on the sparkling vastness. Quiet like the day and soft like the single dusty cloud that floated above, a clump of seaweed rode the swells. Oblivious to storm or calm, the heavy green patch drifted on.

Beaten, drained, injured . . . but still alive, the dark gray petrel sat atop the seaweed, floating wherever the currents would carry him. Captive once again, Lupé was happy just to be breathing, happy to have weathered the storm. He was reminded of a phrase his father had often—perflaps too often—uttered: "Tough birds last longer than tough seas." Lupé grinned.

The seaweed was thick enough to support the petrel, but it was by no means an island. Lupé paced back and forth. He realized he might be trapped where he was for a few days. When his tender wing was rested and healed, he would resume his journey. In the meantime, he wondered how he would feed himself. For the time being, it seemed food would have to come to him. He was in for another lean period, but as long as another storm didn't hit, he was sure he'd be able to make it. He had survived worse than what faced him now.

Lupé decided to examine the seaweed. With a little luck and Pettr's blessing, he might find a few crabs or stowaways. Poking through the leafy green, Lupé came across a clump of black mussels. He loved black mussels. They were one treat the man-flock never provided. The petrel plucked one from the weed, held it firmly in his beak, and jumped into the air. An incredibly sharp pain laced through his side, and he tumbled beak-first into the sea. The mussel slipped free, and with a subtle *plip*, sank toward the bottom.

Lupé climbed back onto the seaweed, realizing that there was no way he could fly, not even a little. Then he smiled as he thought, *Even if I could fly, what would I drop the mussel on to crack it, the water?* Lupé was forced to sit there staring at one of his favorite meals, powerless to feed himself.

The petrel fixed his gaze on the clump of black mussels. He pictured the tender meat inside the tight shell and could almost taste it . . . when his vision waddled away. Lupé was stunned. He had never seen a mussel waddle before. Then another one popped out from under the seaweed, raised its head, and disappeared under a sheet of translucent green.

"Raised its head," Lupé said out loud. "Since when do mussels have heads?"

While he contemplated the bizarre question, a mussel plopped itself down on the petrel's foot. Lupé lowered his head and focused his eyes. Then he understood.

A tiny dark sea turtle spread himself across the webbing between Lupé's toes and prepared to nap in the warm sun. Looking around him, it dawned on the petrel that his seaweed haven was infested with little turtles.

He remembered that he had once asked a large green turtle named Cheekar about this very thing. Lupé had seen turtle eggs, turtle hatchlings, and full grown turtles, but he'd never seen adolescent turtles. One night, he and Cheekar were watching a clutch of young emerge from a sandy nest just off shore. They saw the dainty hatchlings break through the crusty surface and scurry toward the water. Instinctively, the babies chased the light of the moon and the stars that bounced on the sea in front of them.

Occasionally, Lupé would dive at rodents and raccoons who dug up the eggs, or he would chase gull and frigates who tried to pick the young off the beach. Cheekar appreciated Lupé's help, so he told the petrel how turtles spent their mysterious youth. They called it "the hidden years."

Cheekar said, "Those who live long enough to hatch, who can make it to the sea, and who can avoid being eaten by the fish that wait for them, attach themselves to clumps of seaweed. They hide among the floating vegetation until they are large enough to fend for themselves."

So it seemed that Lupé was sharing the seaweed with a group of tiny turtles who were waiting to grow. The petrel laughed. He liked turtles and welcomed their company. He lowered his beak and gently nudged one of the adventurous youngsters off his foot.

Just as the black speck waddled away, the entire clump of seaweed rose and shook. Pieces tore and fell from the edges. Lupé's initial reaction was to think *storm*, but as he looked up at the sky and then scanned the ocean, he could see that all was calm, all except the seaweed he was perched on.

The clump rose again. A hard fin broke through the green and swatted Lupé across its surface. The petrel was terrified. Once again, he was being attacked, and he could not fly. There was no place to hide, no place to protect himself, so Lupé stood motionless on the seaweed and waited for the next strike.

He had seen something like this before. Occasionally, a bird floating on the sea would lose a leg or would actually be swallowed by a passing shark or other fish, but Lupé thought the thick patch of seaweed would hide him from those below. If it was a shark that had spotted him, Lupé knew his chances of survival were slim.

Something burst through the seaweed directly under the bird. Its jaws were stretched wide, and the petrel was caught in between them. Lupé popped into the air. Although he had thrust his body from danger, his legs still dangled beneath. Lupé imagined the pain that would ensue after this shark swallowed one or both of his legs. Would he become a meal, or would he bleed to death stranded on the clump of seaweed? Both these terrible thoughts flew through the petrel's tiny head as he tried to tuck his legs tight against his body.

Then it happened. The jaws slammed shut on one of the bird's legs, and the shark disappeared below. Lupé closed his eyes and waited for the pain. It did not come. *It's probably such a clean cut*, he thought, *that I won't feel anything for a little while, or until the wound becomes infected.* Afraid to look down at what was left of his leg, Lupé searched for the shark or the fish that had done this to him. The creature was gone . . . for now.

He knew he would have to examine the limb, and he forced himself to look down at the bloody stump. As he lowered his head, he closed his eyes. Slowly, reluctantly opening them, the first thing he saw was his foot . . . and it was attached to his leg . . . and his leg was still attached to his body. The petrel bent the limb . . . no pain. He hopped on it . . . still no pain. He examined the other leg. It was fine. Lupé was delighted but puzzled. He had glimpsed the jaws closing on him. There was no way the shark could have missed.

All of a sudden, the pain that Lupé had expected arrived. Well, it wasn't exactly pain. It was more like a severe . . . pinch. Something pinched at the petrel's leg. Then he saw it, just above his ankle. It sparkled in the sunlight, as if Pettr was winking at him. It was the silver band the man-flock had attached to Lupé's leg.

When the shark had tried to remove the bird's feathery supports, he had bitten the hard silver band. Now, slightly bent and twisted, it pinched at the petrel's leg. Lupé leaned over, grabbed it with his beak, and rotated it slightly, and the annoying pinch went away. The petrel sat down on the seaweed, let out a caw of relief, and prepared to thank Pettr for his good fortune . . . but the thanks were premature.

A bulging swell in the water ran against the current. It was headed directly at the clump of seaweed and Lupé. The petrel was too frightened to move. There was nowhere to go. Then out of the ocean rose an enormous green turtle, and it didn't look happy to see Lupé.

The female turtle faced the bird and said, "Now I will do to you what you've done to my young."

Terrified and confused, Lupé shot back, "I haven't done anything to your young."

"Do not lie," the turtle hissed. "It will not save you. I've seen."

"Well, what have you seen?"

"I saw you attack one of my babies." The turtle came closer. "I saw you reach down and attack the one at your feet."

"I did not attack that one or any other!" Lupé screeched. Then he had an idea. "Count your young if you don't believe me."

"And allow you to escape?" the mother questioned.

"There is nowhere I can go."

"You cannot fly?"

"Would I be here if I could?"

The angry turtle studied Lupé, weighing the petrel's words. She finally nodded her glistening, light-brown head and said, "Then I will count my young. Pray that they all are here."

Even though Lupé's life and the life of his entire flock rested on how well this turtle could count, Lupé couldn't help but be amazed at how many young were hidden among the seaweed. A petrel laying anything but a single egg is generally unheard of, but Lupé saw so many baby turtles, he guessed that the mother must have laid well over a hundred eggs to have so many young still alive. Now he realized that all those turtles he saw with Cheek-ar must have come from a single nest. The petrel was impressed.

He waited as the counting continued . . . what else could he do?

"Fourteen, fifteen, sixteen . . ." The big green turtle seemed to know each one by name as she extended a motherly caress to every youngster. And still they emerged from folds in the weed. "Thirty-one, thirty-two, thirty-three . . ."

Lupé waited.

"Forty-seven, forty-eight."

It was over. Lupé felt much better. He had proved his point. Sanity had defeated rage. Now she would know the petrel was no threat to the young turtles.

The mother turned to Lupé and announced, "One seems to be missing."

Lupé's heart stopped. He cried, "No, you must be mistaken. There are so many!"

"I know them all. One is missing. It is Gilgongo, the first to have reached the sea." The turtle paused. Lupé thought he detected a small grin as she said, "Oh, I believe I know where he might be."

"Wonderful," Lupé said, relieved that the mother might find Gilgongo and forget about hurting him.

"Yes," she said, "I think I know precisely where my baby is. I suspect that he's dead and in your belly." The enormous brown head fully extended from its shell. As she pushed herself up on her front fins, her shadow covered the helpless gray petrel.

Very calmly, Lupé reiterated, "I did not harm any of your young."

The fierce turtle snapped back, "I will tear your belly open and find out for myself."

The turtle slid closer.

Lupé heard the slow *shlup-shlup* of large, wet fins slapping the seaweed. But he would not make it easy for her. The petrel did the only thing he could think of, no matter how useless it might prove. He puffed his feathers, lowered his head, and fixed his gaze on the turtle's dark eyes. They were the only vulnerable part of this living rock. If he could attack the eyes, he might be able to protect himself. Unfortunately, directly in front of those eyes were the jaws. Lupé would try to avoid one and strike the other.

The petrel hissed. He had heard a goose do it once and thought it sounded very threatening, but the turtle continued toward him, and the shadow grew darker. She raised her head and opened her powerful jaws.

Lupé felt that even though a quick flap or two would hurt, it might help him move suddenly. He spread his wings wide. The moment he extended them from his flanks, a tiny dark speck fell in front of him and waddled up to the approaching turtle.

Its protector looked down and said, " . . . Gilgongo?"

The black speck raised a minute fin, pointed it at Lupé's wing, and said, "It's soft in there."

The large turtle turned to Lupé. Her expression shifted from motherly relief as she spoke to Gilgongo to outrage. "So, you thought you could hide my baby from me and finish him off later?"

Lupé did not like where this was going. He was about to attempt an explanation when the little one piped up. "He didn't hide me. I hid in him. It really is soft. He has feathers."

Then the mother turtle allowed herself a broad, apologetic smile. She said, "I'm sorry. It appears you were telling the truth after all. Will you forgive me?"

Lupé let out a long breath, folded his wings, and said, as if he could say anything else, "Of course . . . no harm done. I know you were just trying to protect your own. And I also know that there are many birds that prey on your young. But birdsonally, I have never done so."

"Well, that's very nice to hear," the turtle politely responded. "I only wish more birds could say the same."

"Any from my flock could. We were taught to believe that the birds and the turtles are cousins. To the Gwattas, 'turtle' means 'the bird that flies beneath the sea.'"

The reptile added, "And you must be the turtles that swim above the sea?"

Lupé smiled. His brown friend seemed to appreciate petrel logic.

"It's an interesting thought," the turtle mused, "but really . . . look at the two of us. We don't have much in common."

"Not true," Lupé countered. Then, taking stock of his indignation, he continued, "With all due respect, we are far more similar than we are different." He raised the feathers on the back of his neck just as his grandmother used to do during intellectual exchanges. He asked, "What are those things that stick out from under your shell?"

"Only a very stupid bird would not know that these are my fins . . . Are you such a bird?"

Reluctantly, Lupé nodded his head and said, "I confess to being such a bird, because to me, they look like wings."

The turtle grinned.

"And what is that on your face?" Lupé asked.

"It would take an even stupider bird not to know that this is my mouth . . . Are you such a bird?"

Again Lupé nodded his head. He said, "It seems you are in the presence of such a bird, because to me, it looks like a beak."

This time, a little laugh escaped the turtle. It started deep within her shell, bubbled up, and popped out through her fluttering nostrils.

"And how do you bear your offspring?" Lupé had no intention of letting up with anything less than complete acknowledgement from his wet friend.

"Yeees," the mother turtle conceded. "I dig a *nest*. I lay my *eggs*. And I return to the ocean and wait for them to *hatch*."

"Now you get it," Lupé said. "Eggs, nest, beak, wings . . . We are cousins. I can no more harm your young than I can harm my own."

The turtle and the petrel became instant friends. Once again, Pettr had provided. The mother turtle told Lupé her name was Pingolo, but her friends called her Ping. She seemed very pleasant now that her young were safe, and she spent the rest of the day patiently listening to Lupé tell the story of his flock, capture, escape, and now his search.

When he was through, Ping said, "Lupé, you will stay here with my children. I will bring food, and I will drag this seaweed toward the warm water until you are ready to fly. As I protect my own, so shall I protect you."

Lupé had no doubt that Pingolo could provide for and protect him quite adequately. He felt very secure. And since he really had no choice anyway, he accepted the turtle's offer and thanked her for her kindness.

During their conversation, Lupé asked Ping if it was typical for a mother turtle to pay so much attention to her young. Throughout the talk, Ping smiled. It was, perhaps, what Lupé liked best about her. She was naturally happy. If you asked Ping whether an open clam was half empty or half full, she would always see it as half full. She was one of those creatures that tried to enjoy everything life presented to her, but on the other wing, her feelings ran as deep as the ocean she and Lupé floated on.

When the petrel praised the extraordinary care she gave to her young, a faint hollowness replaced her happy glow. The painful grin forced across her tan face was betrayed by the turtle's empty, wet eyes.

Ping said, "This is not the kind of care my mother gave me . . . or the kind of care her mother gave to her. Until now, it was never necessary."

"What do you mean?" Lupé asked. "You have so many young, and they're so healthy . . . I'm sure most of them would do fine even if you didn't worry about them so much. I only wish I was as fortunate as you."

"I also wish you had many young to care for, but things are not always as wonderful as they appear." This time, it was Ping's turn to enlighten.

"I may not be as desperate as you," she continued, "but we are swimming in the same ocean. There are not as many turtles as there once were, and every day, there are fewer."

"But you can add a hundred new lives every year," Lupé pointed out. He looked around at Ping's young playing on the seaweed, and half talking to her, half talking to Pettr, said, "I will be incredibly lucky if I can add just one. And even if I'm so blessed, what will *one* do?"

"True, Lupé, the Greens are not as close to extinction as your flock. I've said that. But just as our beaks are not so different, the same can be said for our problems. Someday, one of mine—Gilgongo, perhaps—may be faced with what challenges you . . . If I did not care for my young as I do and allowed them to progress as Nature originally intended, one or two might survive to adulthood. And given where we are today, that's no longer good enough."

Ping appeared tired and drained, yet at the same time, it seemed that she needed to tell Lupé what troubled her. The petrel did not interrupt. A corner of his mind was busy with thoughts of his own. If one or two surviving young every year was not good enough for the turtles, what did that say about his fate, the Gwatta's fate?

"My birthplace is no more," Ping continued. "Although my soul pulls me to that piece of shoreline, I do not return. I cannot return. It is not safe. My eggs and hatchlings would not survive there. I'm not even sure I could find a patch of undisturbed beach to dig a nest.

"I have been lucky enough to find another spot. Most have not. The clutch, however, faces its greatest danger after I have left the nest and before they have hatched. Many creatures look for the nests and destroy the eggs."

Suddenly, little Gilgongo popped through the leafy weed beneath Ping and said, "When it was time to hatch, we spent three days digging through the egg shell and the sand just to break out of the nest. Then the beach was teeming with us, all covered with sand, all running to the ocean . . . First we encountered loose sand, then it was packed a little harder and we moved faster. When it felt wet underneath us, we pushed ourselves harder than we thought possible.

"Those who were strong and lucky reached the sea. We felt that first salty wave wetting our dry shells. It was an incredible feeling . . . And it was also terrible, Lupé. You begin your life watching too many of your brothers and sisters die . . . But a strange thing happened to some of the other nests on the beach. The eggs were taken by humans, picked up and carried away."

"And killed or held?" Lupé interrupted.

"No," Ping said. "Listen to Gilgongo. It's very strange."

The little turtle continued, unimpressed with the notion that adults were so interested in his story. "The humans took eggs and

sometimes small turtles, but they never harmed them. When the eggs hatched and the little ones grew larger and stronger, they were gently released into the sea. I have spoken to these turtles. Some have joined us on this seaweed."

"It's true," Ping added. "I've seen humans wait on shore and protect the nests from predators. I do not understand it."

Lupé also looked confused when he said, "It is not like the man-flock at all. When I was held by them, it never seemed like they intended to let me go, but it does sound like the man-flock wants to help you."

"Some do," Ping said, but she was quick to include, "some don't. When they strip the sea of fish, humans often take my brothers and sisters as well. Many are not returned."

A very philosophical Gilgongo rubbed a tiny dark flipper across his brow and said, "Maybe . . . Maybe humans are like other creatures. Some are good, and some are bad. Maybe there is mankind and there is also manunkind."

"I think you are right," Ping agreed.

Sour and skeptical from his captivity, Lupé mumbled, "Well, I'm still waiting to see the good ones myself."

While Ping turned to watch her young, Gilgongo slid across the seaweed and climbed onto Lupé's wing. He nestled himself very comfortably beneath the fluffy gray feathers and was sound asleep before Ping spoke her next words.

"I had a mate," she began, and then, nodding to the youngsters racing around the seaweed, added, "obviously."

The petrel wondered what brought on this disclosure and where it would go.

Ping continued, "His name was Jahroo. He survived the nest, the race to the ocean, and the fish that waited for him. He grew large and powerful, and together, we had our babies. When it seemed that Jahroo and I were going to be blessed with each other forever, he was taken from the sea. He swam into the long tentacles of the tiny islands that float across the water, the islands humans use to pull all life from the ocean.

"Jahroo called to me. He warned me to stay away. But the harder he tried to free himself, the more constricting the tentacles became. They wrapped themselves around his body, pinning his fins against his shell. When Jahroo tried to roll himself over, his head became tangled. The tentacles worked their way over his face and down his neck before they started to squeeze tighter and tighter. Jahroo choked and bled.

"Finally, I swam to him. He was exhausted and just stared at me while I tried to bite through. He needed air and could not rise to take a breath . . . Many others were also caught in the tentacles. Most had already perished. I wondered, 'Could the humans on that floating island eat all of these creatures?'

"Just as I was about try to bite through the tentacles a second time, they began to move. Jahroo was being dragged toward the tiny island. We called to each other as I watched my love being ripped from the sea. He stopped calling. Then he was gone. I decided to follow the floating island. It was not long after he broke through the surface that Jahroo was returned to the sea.

"He hit the water with a clumsy splash . . . and sank. There were no marks on him other than those from his entanglement, but he was dead. I watched him sink silently down. His head and fins were limp against the water, and his body swayed and jerked as he sank. It was movement, but it was lifeless, the empty movement of a body without a soul. My heart sank to the bottom of the sea with Jahroo. I will never forget what happened that day. I will never forget the sudden silence of being alone without my mate."

Ping looked so sad, so broken, Lupé did not know what to say. Then he whispered, "I am sorry. I have also lost those who were special to me . . . It is the hardest thing we have to bear."

"I know, Lupé," she said. "What I can't understand is how well you carry the burden. I've lost my love, but you've lost everyone . . . how do you survive the loneliness?"

Without hesitation, Lupé said, "The same way you do. I look to others, to my Lord . . . and I look to myself. I still have me . . . my memories, and the possibility that I will meet another from my flock. Besides, Pettr has a plan for me. He's not done with me yet. I know it."

A half smile returned to Ping's featherless face. She said, "It seems your courage is contagious. Please watch over the little ones. I will be back." The turtle dipped below the surface and disappeared into the murky green.

After a short time, Ping returned with food for Lupé and her young. She did this several times until all had eaten. When the little ones were through, they began to explore Lupé. Ping made sure that there weren't many visitors to the seaweed, so it wasn't often that the youngsters had guests to play with.

But there was another factor that increased Lupé's popularity. Gilgongo made the mistake of telling a few of his siblings how fluffy the petrel was. Word travels fast on a clump of seaweed, so it wasn't long before all forty-nine turtles were climbing over each other, trying to reach Lupé first. Ever so gently, and with an exaggerated laugh just in case Ping was watching, Lupé brushed turtle after turtle from his wings, legs, and rump. *This*, the petrel thought, *is no way to rest up for the last leg of my journey.*

It occurred to Lupé later that evening that Ping had not eaten. When he asked her about it, Ping explained that her appetite was not the problem. Her jaw was sore, so she thought she'd wait until morning to feed.

Lupé thought for a moment. He started to sputter a little giggle. A playful tone emerged as he asked, "Did this problem begin shortly after you tried to have one of my legs for a snack?"

Intrigued, the turtle said, "Yes, it did."

Lupé nodded his head knowingly and proudly proclaimed, "I'll bet you never bit a bird that has legs as hard as mine."

"You know, Lupé . . . while I don't make a habit of biting birds, I could have sworn your skinny leg was in my mouth. Don't misunderstand, I'm glad it wasn't, but I was sure I had it between my jaws."

"You did," Lupé teased.

"But when I snapped them shut, it was like I bit into a clam. Your legs are as hard as coral."

Lupé puffed out his chest feathers and said, "You didn't realize how strong these little legs were, did you?"

Ping looked Lupé in the eyes. Then she whispered, "Do you have special powers?"

Now Lupé laughed uncontrollably. In between sputters, he managed to choke out, "If I had special powers, would I be the last of a flock, stuck on a clump of seaweed . . . with little turtles climbing all over me?" The petrel shook another of the little ones from his tail feathers as he continued to crow. "The only power I have," he added, "is luck and Pettr's blessing."

"Then how the shell did you escape my jaws?" Ping demanded.

"You just happened to bite the silver ring." Lupé stretched out his leg, and the mangled ring flashed in the moonlight.

Now Ping laughed. She told her friend, "After I bit you, my jaws hurt and my head ached . . . I had serious doubts about attacking you again." Ping grinned and confessed, "That's why I waited so long to approach you a second time. I thought you might have powers."

"Well, I'm glad you waited. If you hadn't, little Gilgongo might not have shown up until it was too late for me."

Lupé and Ping extended wing to fin and gently slapped each other as they chuckled on and on. Soon, the little ones came down with giggle fever and chattered along with their mother and guest. The strangest sound on the sea that night was the laughing clump of seaweed as it drifted toward the warm water.

As time passed, Lupé began to feel better. Using Ping's shell for support, he would pop into the air, flap a few times, glide in a circle, and then touch down on his friend's hard back. Ping, happy to see her friend healing so well, would nod her approval. Every day, the petrel would fly a little higher, a little longer. Once or twice, he even managed to bring some tiny fish back to Ping's young. It was a small but genuine attempt to repay what his host had given him.

Early one morning, after Lupé returned with a bountiful beak-full, Ping began to question the petrel about flight. She asked him what it was like to soar above the ocean, to slice through the clouds, to move so swiftly across the planet.

Flight was something Lupé took very seriously, as most birds do. He looked at the turtle and said without pause, "I don't know if you'll understand this, Ping, but I think you might. For me, flight is God. It is Pettr and heaven combined. It is perfection . . . I am never more at peace or closer to Pettr than when I am on the wing. Flight is a prayer instantly heard, immediately answered . . . I am on the other side when I fly."

Ping seemed to drift off a little. She allowed the petrel's words to swim through her mind. Then, slowly, she began to nod. "I understand," she said. "I have not flown with your Pettr, but I know what it's like to swim with God. I have felt perfection under the sea. Gliding silently though pink coral, seeing my little ones grow larger, and feeling the warm current cut across me while I slide through rays of sunlight that pierce the chilling green . . . I understand."

Then Ping had one of those looks on her wet face. It was a look Lupé had seen before. He knew enough about the turtle to be wary

of it. This look usually meant Ping had an idea, a request as unde-
niable as the tide.

Ever so delicately, the mother turtle said, "Lupé, since I would
love to be able to fly with you and I know I never will, would you
consider swimming with me?" Ping's slick head tilted slightly to
one side, and her rear flipper tapped anxiously as she waited for
Lupé's answer.

It was not something the petrel wanted to do. Ping knew this
but pretended she didn't. However, Lupé didn't want to disappoint
his friend. Ping also knew this and pretended she didn't.

The shifty turtle decided a little coaxing was in order, so she
soothed, "Don't worry, I won't let anything happen to you."

Before he committed himself, Lupé thought he should get a
better understanding of what Ping wanted. "Must I go completely underwater?" he probed.

"It would be nice," Ping answered.

When Lupé asked, "How long would I have to do this?" the mot-
tled brown, tan, and black skin that covered Ping's featherless face
creased with joy as the turtle fought the urge to flaunt a shameless
smile. Lupé hadn't consented yet, but Ping was sure she'd get her
way. Her friend would share the sea with her.

Again, the petrel inquired, "How long do you expect me to do
this?"

"Only until you are done," the reptile replied coyly.

"And that will be decided by me, I trust?"

"Of course," the turtle quipped. "Who else would decide such
a thing?"

Lupé agreed to the swim. Then he frowned and said, "I get the
feeling that even though this was my choice, I had nothing to do
with the decision."

As she slipped into the calm sea, Ping dismissed the idea,
laughing. "Don't be silly."

Just as Lupé was transformed when surrounded by sky, Ping
was transformed when immersed in the sea. She became lighter,
quicker, and infinitely more mobile than she was when she crawled

on top of the seaweed. Lupé enjoyed watching Ping lose herself in the ocean.

"Come, Lupé," she called. "You will get wet, but you have been wet before. Come see what I see, feel what I feel. There is nothing to fear. I will protect you."

Certainly, Lupé had been underwater before, but it was usually only for an instant. He would pluck a fish and retreat before a bigger fish plucked him. Now he was going to see firstwing what it was like to be one of those birds who fished like fish.

Lupé gave his oily feathers a hearty shake. Then he wondered why he did it, since soon his plumage would be soaked. He prepared himself and looked for Ping. Lupé had no intention of touching the water unless she was at his side.

His happy companion popped up right in front of him and said, "It is time to become a turtle."

That was all it would take. Lupé thrust himself into the air and climbed high above Ping. Overhead, he flew a silent, lofty circle. Then the petrel tucked his wings to his sides and allowed gravity to do the rest. Lupé split the sea with a subtle *plip*, pushing himself in as deeply as he could.

The first thing the petrel noticed was the pull, the tug all around him everywhere he moved. The water felt like a heavy wind that blew in all directions. Next, he was struck by the vision. On the one wing, he was overwhelmed by the sight of Ping. She circled him, slowly spiraling her entire body. Then she rose abruptly and climbed into a golden shaft of light that shot deep into the pale green.

Lupé could not decide whether Ping swam, flew, or danced. It was undisturbed beauty, pure grace. The turtle seemed to actually attract the light. It appeared to follow Ping as she moved around and through the bending beam.

Lupé appreciated how dark the ocean could be. Beyond and below the light, the sea became pitch. While the sky looked bright and endless, the ocean turned cold, black, and confining. The petrel could not see the curve of the planet, nor did the horizon slip from view as it did among the clouds. Down here, in the deep water, it simply got dark.

For the moment, Lupé gave no thought to air. He found himself paddling, fighting not to rise to the surface, to keep himself submerged so he could concentrate on Ping's performance. Indeed, he marveled at how she used her front fins, flapping them like wings. The rear fins barely moved. She used them to steer the same way Lupé used his tail-feathers. And she used them to design her display.

The turtle disappeared into the black below him. She rose again, up into the shaft of sunlight. Staying inside the ray, she followed it up toward the surface. The light illuminated her head and caused her shell to sparkle. As she passed the petrel, Lupé felt the urge to follow her.

When he paddled into the beam, he was struck by the blinding brilliance. The ocean had intensified and concentrated the glare. It was more than sunlight. It was the rich white of the other side, the glow of forever. Inside the beam, there seemed to be no water. Lupé tried to breathe. Then he heard it.

The voice of Pettr spoke a single word: "Sun." As the petrel continued his ascent up the shaft of light, he heard the word again:

"Sun." Bathed in light, Lupé wasn't sure what was happening. He felt dizzy and thought he might be drowning or perhaps imagining it all. Suddenly, he felt Ping beneath him. The turtle gently nudged her friend to the surface.

Lupé was choking when he broke through the water. He climbed onto the seaweed and coughed up torrents of salty sea while the little turtles squeaked with laughter. Soon, Lupé began to breathe without much trouble. Ping did nothing to help. She merely swam around the seaweed, waiting for Lupé to gather himself. When the petrel appeared fully recovered, Ping coyly asked, "Did you enjoy your swim?"

There was no mistaking Lupé's foul mood when he stomped toward the turtle and said, "Oh yes, I love a good brush with death . . . although lately, it seems to be the story of my life."

"So you are disappointed?" Ping inquired.

"Disappointed?" Lupé repeated. "I nearly met my maker down there!"

Lupé was about to deliver a very colorful beak-lashing when he began to recall what had happened before the water had overtaken him. His anger with Ping vanished. He remembered flying high, entering the sea, watching Ping perform some type of dance . . . His mind locked on the dance.

"Ping," Lupé said, "what were you doing before, when we were in the sea together?"

"Swimming," she said.

"No, it was different. It was more than that . . . What were you doing?"

Ping's expression remained intact, but she stopped circling the seaweed. Lupé noticed a glow, a glimmer in her eyes. He heard the turtle mutter under her breath, "It worked."

Without the petrel having to ask again, Ping explained that her display was a dance, a sacred dance turtles performed for special friends. Ping said she had never heard of the dance being done for one who was not a turtle, but since Lupé had become so dear to her, and since he had pointed out how closely related turtles and birds are, Ping thought she'd see what effect the display might have on him. She explained that her performance was intended to mesmerize the observer, to help the witness come closer to the spirit of the planet, the part of the soul that lived in everything, the spark of life.

Lupé was astonished. He told Ping about his experience.

"It is fitting," she said.

The petrel remembered the warm ray of sun, Pettr's eye looking deep into the sea, searching for Lupé and Ping. He recalled that even though he was well underwater, when he looked up the beam, he could see directly into the clear sky. There was no distortion at all. It was as though the sea did not flow through the light.

Then he remembered the word *Sun*. Lupé knew immediately that it was the next step in the mantra of the birds of pray. Pakeet, his savn grandmother, had provided the first clue, *Sea*. Now Pettr had seen fit to add the next word himself. Lupé wondered if this meant that he was getting closer, or maybe falling behind.

He was lost in thought. He completely forgot about Ping. But the turtle didn't mind. On the contrary, she hoped something like this might happen.

The introspective bird was flooded with ideas. He was happy, because this showed that Pettr was still watching over him. And since Pettr had provided the next word in his mantra, Lupé believed his Lord was pleased with him. What had happened to him under the water could only be interpreted as encouragement from above. But Lupé believed there was something more to the message. It was a signal, a warning perhaps. Pettr was telling him to move on, to find the Islands of Life, and get on with it.

The petrel told the turtle his analysis of the events. Ping was excited that the display had exceeded her expectations, but at the same time, she was saddened by the thought of losing her new friend.

It was time for Lupé to fly. He told Ping that once he hit the warm water, he would cross the thin stretch of land that separated the Smaller Ocean from the Ocean of Peace. Then he hoped Pettr, or the wind, or something would lead him to the islands. Ping had never heard of the islands before. She was sure they were not in the Smaller Ocean, but the petrel already knew as much.

Lupé thanked Ping for all her help. He rubbed his beak against her neck and called her by her full name, Pingolo. The two wished each other luck. Neither was especially skilled at farewells. They took one long last look to feed the memory and warm the soul. Then Lupé popped into the air. Once again, he was on the wing.

The golden-green seaweed grew smaller and smaller as Lupé climbed higher into the sky. But while the meandering patch was still in sight, he heard Ping and a chorus of small turtles, led by Gilgongo's distinctive squeak, wishing him well.

Carried by the wind and the turtle's melody, Lupé began the next part of his journey. He thought about how lucky he was, and he sent his thanks to Pettr.

Part Three

Bird Meets Girl

Long after the melody of the turtles echoed in his mind, Lupé came to a relatively thin stretch of land commonly referred to as the Neck. Sea birds called it that based on a legend that was as old as the first flock.

The legend claimed that the man-flock would one day become more powerful than the planet itself. There would be so many of them doing the same things that the man-flock would, in effect, become a single massive creature. The beast's head would lie in the enormous land mass above the warm water. Below would be the body, the southern landmass where the man-flock would strip the Earth to feed itself and its head to the north. The neck, which is where Lupé now flew, was the thin length of land that connected the head and the body.

Lupé crossed quickly. The anxious bird felt strong, rested. His wings worked well as he slid through the sky with ease. He wondered why he suddenly felt so good. Then he realized his body sensed how close he was to Peace. Lupé had finally returned to the sea of his birth. It greeted him with sunshine, clear water, and a soft breeze. The happy petrel dove beak-first into the friendly sea.

The instant Lupé surfaced, salt water still rolling off his feathers, he heard, "You're doing it all wrong."

The petrel saw the shadow of a very large bird circling him. Then he heard again, "Young bird, I say, you're doing it all wrong."

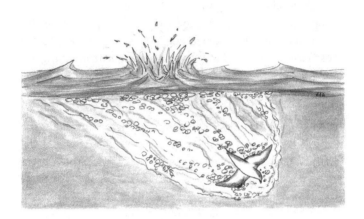

The uninvited guest, a weather-worn albatross, selected a spot on the sea and splashed down next to Lupé. The mature male was white with gray splashes. He bore an impressive yellow beak and incredibly long, thin wings. When it came to sheer distance, there was not another bird on the sea that could rival the albatross. Lupé knew of some that went years without ever touching actual soil. The creature that sat across from him was definitely a bird of the sea.

"My word, you're doing it all wrong," the albatross insisted a third time, and then he added, "Horrifying technique."

"Eggsactly what am I doing wrong?" Lupé questioned.

"Why, fishing—plunge diving, specifically. Lesson number one: It's not wise to fish unless there happen to be fish present."

"I'm not fishing," Lupé explained.

"Oh, of course you are. It's nothing to be ashamed of, young hen."

"I'm not a young hen."

"Oh, do forgive me," the albatross apologized. "I'm quite sorry, indeed. I had absolutely no idea. You could knock me over with a feather. It's just that compared to me, you do seem rather young, actually quite youthful, I must say. You do carry your age exceedingly well. And what a fine figure of a mature female you are, if you don't mind my saying so."

Lupé minded. He did not know what bothered him more, having his gender mistaken, or the suggestive look in the lonely albatross's eyes. The petrel was forced to point out something he'd thought he'd never have to. He said, "I am a male."

Contrite but tickled nonetheless, the albatross replied, "Indeeeed . . . Oh, I am exceedingly sorry for my lack of perception. I should have recognized your splendid maleness immediately. It's just that my eyes have been getting a little too much *sea sun* lately."

The last few words passed Lupé without notice, since he was extremely eager to explain the other bird's oversight. The petrel graciously said, "It's quite all right. I am not a very common bird, although others tend to mistake only my flock."

"Well, I know you'll find this hard to believe, but I am ever so slightly—just a touch, mind you—nearsighted. Now that I can observe you closer, it's quite obvious that you're an exceptional example of your gender . . . a fine example, indeed."

"Thank you very much." Lupé was reassured and pleased that the other bird had misidentified his sex based solely on an admitted visual defect. However, his concern resurfaced when he noticed that the longing, lonely look in the albatross's eyes had not completely disappeared.

Desperate to change the subject, Lupé continued, "What were you saying before about my doing it all wrong?"

"Why, fishing. Please forgive the presumption, but if I may . . ." And without pausing for Lupé's consent, the albatross pressed on, "The most basic fundamental of fishing is that there be fish in the water. And this location is obviously barren at the moment. Now, if you're looking for a meal and you'd rather not wait for the proper tide, I would be happy to—"

"Thank you," Lupé interrupted, "but I really wasn't fishing."

"No need to make things up, chickie. Don't be embarrassed. Of course you were fishing."

"No, I really wasn't."

"Then, pray tell, why were you diving in and out of the water? I suppose you were doing it for fun?"

"Yes, that's exactly what I was doing." Lupé went on to explain that he had been away from the Ocean of Peace a long time and was merely celebrating his return. He told the albatross that he was searching for the Islands of Life and asked the well-traveled bird if he knew anything about them.

The nautical wayfarer took a deep breath and said, "Well, I've been at sea long enough to have seen every corner of the ocean twice, and I can tell you without fear of contradiction that these islands you seek . . ." He took a second prolonged breath, nodded several times, and resumed, "These islands, yes . . . might just be out there, somewhere."

It was at this point that Lupé knew there was no such thing as a simple answer from the albatross. So he said goodbye to the bird and prepared to continue his search. When he was just about to fly off, he heard the bird say, "Search wherever you like, sweetwings. It is a big ocean, but you might want to start with Galahope."

Lupé's first reaction was to fly on, but something kept him where he was. He asked, "Where and what is . . . Galahope?"

"Oh, so now you're interested? No longer in a rush?" The albatross floated on the sea preening at his feathers. Eventually, he cleared his throat, swallowed deeply, and said, "It happens to be a group of small islands—an archipelago, if you will—more than a dozen islands clustered below the warm water."

"Where below the warm water? And why do you think I should go there?"

"On second thought, I'm not so sure you should. You appear to be independent. You're obviously your own bird. And I get the impression you're somewhat solitary, a loner like myself. So you might not be interested after all."

Lupé screeched, "I'm interested! I'm interested!"

"Well, no need to raise one's voice. The only reason I mentioned it at all is that on one of these islands, a larger one, I saw an entire colony of birds—petrels, in fact—exactly like yourself. It is the only place I've ever seen your kind . . . but you would probably prefer to be on your own, wouldn't you?"

"Eggsactly where is Galahope?" Lupé pressed, ignoring the tone and taunts from the large bird.

"Let's see, from where we float now . . ."

The petrel waited anxiously.

" . . . from this spot, I would estimate . . . It's been quite some time for me . . . but I would surmise . . . oh, a few days' flight south by southwest from where we float, and a fair distance off the big western shore of the Body. Maybe another two days' flight into the setting sun—depending on the wind, of course."

Lupé looked in the direction the albatross suggested. It looked like an easy flight for a petrel, and he could probably get there in less time than it took to get the directions, he thought. He was ready to go.

He turned back to thank the loquacious explorer who floated next to him . . . but the albatross was gone. There were no ripples, feathers, or any other markings where the visitor had sat on the sea. Lupé looked up. The sky was empty . . . Then he spotted him high above the clouds. Carried by bold strokes, the albatross headed toward the sun. It was much too far for him to have gone in the short time Lupé had looked away. Although albatrosses could fly great distances, they were not quick. Then the feathered speck disappeared into the light.

While Lupé flew on toward Galahope, he thought about the albatross. He wondered what the bird's name was, and whether he actually entered the sun or was merely shrouded by its glare. Lupé also thought about what he might find on the islands. Would there actually be a flock of his kind?

Because he was so heavy in thought and so full of hope, the time passed quickly. He pumped his wings with renewed vigor. Reaching the Ocean of Peace was one thing, but now that he was flying to what might be his flock, Lupé sliced through the sky with no trouble at all. He flew on through the night, the day, the night, the day, the night, concentrating carefully on what lay below.

As first light began to fade the night, Lupé saw something he
liked. The water underneath him had become surf. It was breaking against land. He could see a ring of what looked like tiny snow-
capped mountains, rolling and disappearing, erupting in white
where the green sea slapped gray rock. He had come to a group of
islands.

Lupé circled the great mounds of dried lava that had flowed
from active volcanoes, which were now dormant craters. It was
still dark, but as dawn wore on, he would be able to see more. Soon,
he would be able to begin his exploration. But he was in unfamiliar surroundings. He understood the importance of caution. He
remembered how he was rewarded by the man-flock when he dove
blindly into a crevice to answer a female's call, so he flew carefully, waiting for light to fill the sky.

Gazing at the islands below him, Lupé was reminded of the
vision he had had in the silver web. Were these the islands Pettr
had shown him? Lupé tried to recall the details of the dream. He
hated to do it, but he tried to put himself back inside the web. He
listened to the sounds of the wind and the surf, felt the dawn, and
chanted, "*Sea, Sun . . . Sea, Sun . . . Sea, Sun . . .*" Lupé hoped that the

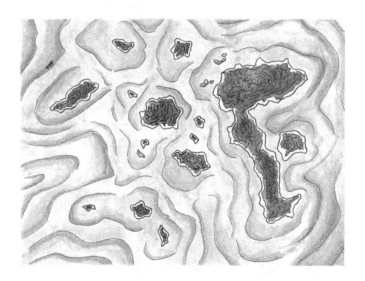

words would carry his questions to Pettr as he concentrated on the islands below. But the petrel could not recreate the vision in the web, and Pettr did not respond to his prayer. Lupé knew he would have to find his answer another way.

The petrel shifted his attention to the foaming surf that surrounded the islands. He heard the cutting fizz and could feel the crisp spray of the chilly water. Although it was a warm locale, cold currents flowed here, bringing food and life. *Maybe these are the islands*, he thought.

Soon, Lupé was soaring through the low clouds that were so wet, the petrel could almost drink the wind. He descended onto the rim of a massive crater and perched so that he overlooked the shore. The sun rose and warmed his plumage. Wind shook the scrubby trees that grew inland. The petrel turned away from the sea and looked into the brush. Then he glanced down at the earth that spawned the vegetation and asked himself, "Could this be home?"

A dusty spray of dirt and sand flew up from the stone where he stood and into the petrel's eyes. He shook his head, ruffled his feathers, and flapped his wings just as he always did when sprayed with dirt. The grains that fell from his feathers captured his attention. He brushed them with his foot, and the wind blew them back. Lupé turned so that the wind was behind him and brushed again. The soil returned and continued to blow in no matter how Lupé positioned himself until two small piles covered the petrel's webbed feet. Although it was not the way wind behaved normally, Lupé was not afraid.

The mounds of dirt that held him to the stone warmed and welcomed him. The wind was telling him something. When Lupé stepped from the tender grasp of the grains piled on his feet, he knew that the third word to his savn mantra was *Soil . . . Sea, Sun, Soil*. Pettr did not have to tell him. The wind and the island delivered the message. Galahope and the Islands of Life were one and the same. *Sea, Sun, Soil . . .* this was the soil. He stood on the aged lava and studied the terrain of his new home.

Looking out at the sun rising over a stand of dwarf trees, Lupé noticed a group of birds in flight. Judging from their shape and their erratic flapping, he knew they could only be one type of bird—petrels!

Lupé studied them as they flew closer. What type of petrels were they? A female passed, followed by one, two, three, four, five, six excited youngsters. And all of them looked like Lupé! The petrel was overjoyed. He watched them flying together. It was one of the most beautiful sights he had ever seen. He had always hoped to find a female, but never did he dream there would be a flock. The words of the albatross came back to him, " . . . an entire colony, exactly like yourself."

It was magnificent. Things Lupé didn't dare imagine were coming true. But by the time he realized he should fly over and introduce himself, the other petrels were gone. Lupé was so caught up in the joy of the moment, the gaggle had flown by and continued on their way. Since he had found them once, he decided it wouldn't be difficult to find them again. Galahope wasn't *that* big.

A melody from Lupé's distant past rose from somewhere on the island—cackles, screeches, tooting, squawking, bird-like barking, wings flapping, guttural chuckling—thousands of birds united in a bizarre harmony, many flocks living together. The island was rich with activity, yet blended in with the wonderful cacophony of bird life were those unique sounds Lupé had heard as a hatchling, the sounds of *his* flock. It had to be the colony the albatross spoke of. Lupé tried to isolate the din of the gathering. He followed the distinctive jabber as though it were a current in the air. It carried him.

The petrel glided past the shore, above the dense thorn-brush thicket, and over a second weathered volcanic ridge. From the distance, he saw them. The sky was thick with sea birds, many of them petrels. Sunlight flickered through flocks of flapping wings and darting bodies.

Below, the aerial bustling petrel pairs nested in burrows spread out among stunted pines, oaks, and cacti. These had to be the Islands of Life. Lupé's vision was finally realized. He saw before him a happy, healthy flock of petrels just like him. Several downy chicks hopped and tripped around their holes. There could never be a sight more beautiful than this, he thought, unless of course—dare he even think it—there would one day be chicks of his own.

Lupé landed on the branch of a tall, leafless shrub. He was not quite sure what to do next. Looking down into the burrows, he glimpsed the speckled splendor of new life, petrel eggs yet unhatched. And then it struck him, covering Lupé like a wave that rose from the sea and swallowed him. He looked closer, and he knew it was true. What he saw before him were certainly petrels, but they were not his flock.

No doubt they were incredibly similar, but they were not Gwattas. He recalled the nearsighted albatross and smiled sadly to himself. *Yes, a little too much sea sun for the old bird,* he thought. Even Lupé, who was not at all nearsighted, had made the same mistake. Blinded by desperation, he had allowed himself to be overcome by hope.

The longer Lupé looked, the more obvious the differences became. These petrels did not have white wing bars or a pale belly like Lupé. They carried a little more white on their foreheads and cheeks, but the rest of their plumage was even darker than Lupé's. And where all in his flock had split tails, these petrels had rounded rumps. All in all, they were remarkably like Lupé—indeed, the closest he'd ever seen to himself—but the inescapable truth was that they were not his flock. They were not Gwattas.

Just as Lupé came to grips with the unpleasant reality of the situation, he sensed danger. Off to one side in the dry brushwoods, something watched him. Lupé studied the thicket. A petrel hopped out and stared at him. Then another popped out. Two more landed on either side of him. Without expression, they watched Lupé. Outnumbered and unsure, Lupé became alarmed. For some reason, his cousins did not seem happy to see him.

One of the larger petrels landed directly in front of Lupé. He had the confidence of a leader. The bird, who silently studied Lupé, had a chipped, crooked beak. Bristly quills rose on his head and covered his back. His plumage looked pointy and painful to touch, not smooth at all. The bird's feathers reminded Lupé of the dry needles that grew on the island's cactus.

Looking at the group that now surrounded him, Lupé thought, *Bird, am I in trouble.*

One of those that flanked him spoke up. "Who are you?"

Lupé turned to him.

"What flock are you from? And why were you watching us?"

Lupé flashed a friendly grin with hopes that it would bring one back as he replied, "There's no need to worry about me. I am a Gwatta petrel, and my flock has all but passed on. I'm no danger to you. I'm not even sure where I am right now."

"I do not believe you," one from the brushwood said.

"Quiet, Wohat," the large bird in front ordered. "Let the visitor speak."

Lupé took his cue. "Really, I mean you no harm. Actually, I'm very happy to meet petrels so much like myself. I was hoping I might be able to stay with your flock while I decide where to go next."

The leader looked at Lupé, paused, and said, "Decide now and be on your way."

One of the others, who stood on some trembling, loose rocks, suggested, "Maybe we should speak with Tapao? He might find this petrel interesting."

Wohat, the one from the brushwood, flew by and cuffed the petrel who spoke. "Bog will decide what should be done."

Bog was the leader perched in front of Lupé. He was pleased that the visitor saw who controlled punishment here. He said, "You may be interested in us, but we are not interested in you. And that's really what matters here."

If there was one thing Lupé hated, almost as much as a rodent, it was an unfriendly creature. *Unpleasantness is unnecessary*, Lupé thought. *This is a rude bird.* The lone petrel was getting a little angry, a little foolish. He looked at the others who were waiting for their leader's instructions. Then, in a very loud whisper, Lupé told Bog, "One who needs others to enforce his will is usually not worth listening to. I am also not interested in you, but I am curious about this island, so I think I'll stay."

Hate lined Bog's eyes. It was a cold, breathless moment.

Bog wiped his beak with the underside of his wing and shook the mandible as a warning. A challenge was being issued, and lines were being drawn. The leader said, "Stay on this island if you like, but stay away from my flock. You do not belong. Do not test me on this, outsider."

Lupé considered the situation. Bird to bird, he would enjoy accepting Bog's challenge, but to do so now would be ill advised. He had learned long ago never to fight a bird at its own nest. And this was definitely Bog's nest. Also, Lupé understood that he had much more to lose. It would not be wise to wager a race against a life. This was, however, a challenge that would not be forgotten.

He hated to do it, but Lupé relaxed his feathers and lowered his head in a submissive posture. Bog's chest swelled while death remained in his eyes. Lupé caught those eyes in his own, and with bowed beak sent Bog a silent message that he hoped was understood, "I, too, am not to be pushed."

It was time to find a nesting site. Given his recent reception, Lupé knew he'd have to choose carefully. He'd have to find a location that would keep him away from his inhospitable cousins. Even though he was depressed that the petrels were not from his flock, Lupé was encouraged by the fact that there were so many so similar to himself. If he was able to locate these birds, maybe another petrel from his flock might do the same.

Lupé wondered whether Pettr was sending a female to the islands at this very moment. Also, Lupé could not ignore the fact that the third word of the mantra had come to him when he touched down. The more he thought about it, the more determined he was to stay.

The petrel hoped the entire flock would not be as hostile as those he had just met. So he decided to select a site that was outside the colony but still close enough that he might make some friends and get some information. Actually, he really wasn't the type of bird to live in a large colony anyway. He knew that the strength of many wings often created the problems of many nests. He would do as he had always done, go it alone.

Not far from the ragged jagged shoreline, Lupé found a spot that pleased him. Sitting on loose stones, sheltered by a broad green branch, Lupé could hear the steady *thrump-fizz, thrump-fizz* of the ocean striking the shore. He listened to the song of the surf. The heartbeat of the planet pulsed soothingly on. This was where he'd stay, just beyond the outskirts of the colony. He was close enough to be aware, yet distant enough to be undisturbed.

Shaded by a little tree, Lupé considered his next decision: nest or burrow? Since the low branches and scattered rocks already buried him somewhat and since he was hatched in a nest, the choice, although not in keeping with most petrels, was an easy one. So Lupé strolled the area surrounding his new home collecting leaves, twigs, seaweed, shells, stones, and feathers. The petrel used them all to create a hopeful little nest for himself—sturdy, soft, and a snug fit for two feathered rumps.

Almost done, Lupé needed one more twig to weave into the side of his structure. He scoured the ground for the perfect piece. And then he found it, draped over a bare rock just above his head. Not at all brown or brittle, this twig was green and supple. It would be very easy to work into the nest, where it would dry out and harden in place. Lupé stretched his neck, opened his beak, and snapped the twig from the stone.

As he carried it back to his nest, the twig began to twitch and move in his beak. *This feels softer than wood, even green wood*, he thought.

Lupé dropped the twitching twig in front of him and slowly walked back to the boulder to see if some strange moving plant grew there. He came to the rock but saw nothing. He flapped his wings in an effort to get a better view. When his head cleared the large stone, the petrel was shocked to see a marine iguana draped across the rock sunning himself. The lizard who stared back at Lupé just happened to be missing the tip of its rather long tail. It was the lumpiest, bumpiest creature Lupé had ever seen.

The reptile cocked his head and said one word. "Yo."

Still conscious of the last reception he received, Lupé carefully replied, "Hello." After what felt like a migration, the petrel peeped, "You seem to be missing a bit of your tail."

The lizard politely nodded his head, paused, and calmly quipped, "Yub, ya jusdt dore id from my rear ent."

"I'm really sorry," Lupé said. "I was building a nest, and—"

"I know," the reptile interrupted. "My dail loogket ligka dwig. Id's habbent before. Id'll grow bagck. Den I'll tagke anudda nab, ant some birt'll rib id off again. Fuhgeddaboudit, dad's jusdt da way id is."

"I'm really sorry. I had no idea. Do you want me to get your tail for you?"

"Nah, don'd feel bat. Da pain is only incredubly eggscruciatint' for dat instand ya bide my flesh and den rib my dail from da mosd sensudive pard'a my botty. Oddawise, id's no big deal. By da way, my name's Stithl."

Since there was something sourly humorous about Stithl and since it seemed they were living in the same general area, the petrel decided to perch himself and shoot the breeze with the lizard. As they spoke, the irony did not escape Lupé that on Galahope, those who were so similar to himself saw only differences, and yet one so different as the iguana could be so accepting.

Lupé observed delicately, "You have a somewhat unique accent, if you don't mind my saying so."

"Ya dingk?" the lizard said, puzzled by the statement.

"It's interesting, amusing to hear."

"I amuse you? You dingk I'm funny?" Stithl seemed to be getting annoyed, approaching anger.

Lupé consoled him, "No, no, not 'funny.' Not ha, ha. Not at all. I mean interesting. Your expression is unique."

Stithl smiled proudly. "Dad's righd, I'm compledly uniq."

After they ended their chat, Lupé flew down to the shoreline. The water was so clear, it was difficult to tell where the ocean began and where the sky ended. It was such a beautiful setting and Lupé had so much on his mind, he decided to pray.

The petrel relaxed, stood near the surf, and turned his body to face the wind. He ran the three words over in his mind: *Sea, Sun, Soil . . . Sea, Sun, Soil.* Then he tucked one leg against his body, balanced on the other, and swayed in the breeze. It was a strange sensation. On the one wing, he felt like he was gliding, but on the other, he was still firmly planted on the Earth.

A shadow passed across the inside of Lupé's eyelids, breaking his concentration. He continued to pray but opened one eye. He saw a solitary petrel from the colony walking along the shore picking at seaweed. The bird did not appear to be one of those with Bog, so Lupé closed his eye and went back to what he was doing.

Soon, he opened the eye again and took a second look. The bird resembled the female he had seen when he first arrived at Galahope, the one flying out to sea with the young.

She was alone now. She went to a rock, popped up on top of it, and turned into the wind. It looked to Lupé like she, too, had come to pray, although she was not nearly as formal about her meditation as he was. This bugged him a bit. The next thing Lupé knew, he was shouting at her to lift one of her legs.

Lupé called, "You'll get much better results if you lift—" As he stepped toward her, Lupé forgot that his own leg was still tucked away, and he fell flat on his beak. When he tried to push his leg out so that he could stand up, the appendage spasmed and cramped, which caused Lupé to roll toward the surf. His leg finally relaxed, but when Lupé stood and shook the sand from his feathers, a small wave crashed over him and dragged the drenched petrel across loose stones out to sea.

Choking and wet, Lupé realized, "I must look like a real squid." But the worst of it was, Lupé thought he heard the female giggling as she flew away. As embarrassed as he felt, Lupé couldn't help but admire her flight. She flew very nicely. Since she didn't seem at all surprised by his difference, Lupé wondered if perhaps she'd seen a Gwatta petrel before. He decided that the next time he saw this bird, he would speak to her. Then Lupé remembered what an auspicious first impression he must have made and thought, *With my luck, she's probably Bog's mate.*

For the first time in his life, the petrel realized that even if he did meet a female from his own flock, she might not want him. He had never considered the possibility that he might have to impress her. He had always assumed that they would fall for each other the moment they met. An expression—never directed at him, of course —that he had heard several times as a youngster rang in his ears: "I wouldn't have you if you were the last bird on Earth." Since, in a sense, Lupé was the last bird on Earth, this was not an attitude he wanted to encounter.

Soon after he returned to his nest, Stithl slithered over for a visit. He began with, "Yo." Then he asked, "Whud wus dad before?"

"What was what?"

"Dad disblay ad da shoreline."

"Oh, you saw that?"

"All of id." Stithl smiled. "Every bid, from when ya began ta pray ta when ya call't ta da female ta when ya fell on ya beagk ta when ya god wash't oud, ta—"

"Okay," Lupé interrupted. "I know what happened. I was there. No need to relive it."

There was silence. Lupé welcomed it.

Stithl, however, cocked his head and asked, "D'ya mindt if I magke a liddle obsavashun?"

Lupé definitely minded, and he hoped the tailless iguana would get the hint when he said, "You've already observed plenty."

Stithl did get the hint . . . and ignored it. The lizard's bumpy head bobbed rhythmically as he said, "Lubé, ya nod smoot."

"What do you mean, I'm not 'smoot'?" the defensive petrel challenged.

"We doan really know each odda very well, so I'm dryin' ta be tagtful, bud how can ya possibly imbress a female by loogkin' ligka complede squit?"

Lupé caught himself saying, "I knew I looked like a . . ." Then he gathered his composure and said, "I was not trying to 'impress' anyone. I just noticed that . . . that 'bird' was praying with poor technique."

"She wasn'd da only one wid poor tegchneegque . . . jussd sayin'. Loogk, Lubé, dis is me, Stithl, ya talgkin' ta. I've seen id all.

I know whud's goin' on. Id don' madda whedda ya a rebdile or a birt. Neets is neets. So doan give me any'a dis praya tegchneegque stuff."

Lupé was getting mad. "What are you suggesting? Listen here, you lumpy lizard. Don't tell me what's going on in my mind. I know what happened down there."

"Yeah, so da I. Ya fell on ya beagk, god hid by a wave, an' god dragg't agross rogks oud ta sea. Ligke I sait, smoot."

Lupé was never so tempted to just blast another creature with hot oil. He could feel the liquid welling up behind his beak, just itching to spray the smug iguana, to cover his dark green face with sticky orange, but the petrel refrained.

Stithl, however, had no idea what was flying through Lupé's mind and had no intention of refraining. "Lubé," he said with a slight grin, "ya know, I wuz wondrin', if ya sugch a rare pedrel, is id safe ta say ya neva been wid a female before? Don'd dagke id da wrong way. I'm jussd asgkin'."

This was not a topic Lupé wanted to discuss with anyone, especially Stithl. He decided he wouldn't say anything until the lizard could find a topic worth discussing.

All Stithl said was, "Yeah, dad's whud I wuz afrait'a. Well, I'm here if ya eva neet'a lizart ta gcry on."

Lupé thought, *Why couldn't I have ripped his tongue out instead of his tail?*

That evening, Lupé was visited by Tapao, the leader of the petrel colony. Tapao came alone. He seemed a little older than Lupé, the kind of bird who could be gentle and strong at the same time. He was also much friendlier than Bog. The leader explained that Bog did not speak for the entire flock, and he was quick to add, "No one bird can speak for all."

After they visited a short time, Tapao invited Lupé to live in the colony if he wanted to. Lupé appreciated the offer, but said he would rather stay where he was. Lupé was comfortable and thought the others would be more comfortable with him if he appeared gradually. As he explained his thoughts, Lupé noticed a look of relief relax Tapao's brow.

Not sure if he'd even get an answer, the petrel asked, "What is Bog's role with the flock? Is he a problem?"

Tapao replied, "Yes and no. Bog defends the colony and looks out for possible trouble. He and his group are valuable. They can be very tough on our enemies. Unfortunately, they assume that any creature not of our flock is automatically an enemy. They tend to take themselves and their responsibilities a little too seriously and sometimes cause more trouble than they clear up.

"Bog needs to learn," Tapao continued, "that a bird who constantly flies into the wind doesn't usually get anywhere."

"Judging from that chipped beak of his," Lupé said, "it seems Bog spends a lot of time proving himself."

"Well," Tapao replied, "having a battle-scarred beak can be a deterrent or an invitation to a challenge. If it's a deterrent, it can be very useful, but if the beak becomes an invitation, then you don't know how to carry it."

Since it didn't seem Tapao was in any hurry to leave, Lupé kept talking. He found out that Tapao's flock was not originally from Galahope. His flock, who referred to themselves as Darums, left the Islands of Black Sand from the northwest when they lost their nesting sites to the man-flock. The Darums were happy on Galahope, probably one reason why they could be so overprotective.

At first, Lupé thought Tapao was a rather ordinary looking petrel, especially considering he was a leader. Not overly large or aggressive, not very old, not very young, not very striking—Tapao was plain. But as they spoke, Lupé began to see why Tapao was so highly placed. He was honest, and he was wise. Although many take those qualities for granted—often those who don't possess them—these are two of the best things any creature could hope to be. It was obvious to Lupé that Tapao flew the good flight.

Lupé noticed Tapao looking at the silver band around his ankle. Every bird knew what such a thing meant. So Lupé asked the leader if it bothered him, knowing that he had been held by the man-flock. The leader shrugged and said, "The man-flock take who they want. It doesn't tell me anything about you as a bird."

That was when Lupé decided to tell Tapao his story. As patient as a pine, the leader listened to the entire tale. When the younger petrel was through, Tapao surprised him.

"We had a mutual friend," the Darum said.

Immediately, Lupé wondered whom they both might have known. Certainly not Zomis. Ping? Jopi maybe. But Lupé was grounded by what Tapao said next.

"I remember your grandmother, Pakeet."

Lupé's perspective of Tapao instantly shifted. He saw the petrel through different eyes and realized how old he actually was. Tapao was a very old bird that looked like an ordinary middle-aged petrel. The ends of Tapao's dark feathers were thin and faded to the color of fog in the afternoon, but other than that, it was almost impossible to guess the petrel's age. Lupé found this quite amusing. Then it sank in. Here was a bird who had known his grandmother.

"Tell me about her," Lupé said.

"I will be happy to," Tapao said with a smile. "But not tonight."

Although he was just hatching to find out, Lupé did not press. Tapao seemed reluctant to go any further, so he would wait. The leader rose and stretched his wings to leave. But before he left, Tapao explained that there was a group of young Darums who met with an instructor almost every day. He asked if Lupé would consider telling the group about his experiences with the whales. Tapao wanted the youth to learn as many different feeding techniques as possible. The leader guessed that in the future, feeding might not be so easy. The greater knowledge might help feed the flock one day.

Lupé agreed right away. He liked youngsters and thought this would be a good way to show the flock he was no threat.

The petrel's enthusiasm pleased Tapao. He told Lupé to fly away from the rising sun and he would find the group in deep water over the cold current.

The two parted with good feelings between them. Tapao impressed Lupé as an old sky-faring soul, packed with charm and wisdom. He believed he could learn from the soft-spoken leader and hoped Tapao would soon tell him more about meeting Pakeet. After the Darum had gone, Lupé wondered who the flock would fly with if peck ever came to bite, Tapao or Bog? One was the type of bird who inspired; the other made you afraid.

Next morning, Lupé left very early to find the site where the youngsters gathered to learn. When the tip of the sun peeked over the sea, Lupé was already on the wing. Having flown for some time without seeing any others, the petrel became concerned. Was this some kind of trick? Did the Darum leader want to lure Lupé out to sea and then attack him? No, the petrel did not think he had misjudged Tapao. Then it occurred to him that he might just be too early. Lupé turned back to Galahope, hoping to stumble upon the group as they flew out to sea.

And stumble he did. Lupé was intercepted by two young petrels from the Darum flock. They were flying with the reckless abandon of one who is still testing the limits of her wings. The youngsters plummeted from above, attempting to criss-cross in front of Lupé. It was a perfect example of what sea birds call "sealing." The birds know there isn't a bigger show-off on the planet than a seal.

Unfortunately, one of the two decided to criss rather than cross. They struck wings and fell flapping and spiraling into . . . Lupé, who tumbled for a moment but regained himself just in time to see the youngsters crash with a splash.

They came up choking and laughing, an adolescent pair who looked to be brother and sister.

"Radical seal!" the brother screeched.

"Yeah, proper dip!" The sister laughed. "But we better get back."

"Sirka won't be happy with us." The brother thought for a moment while they floated on the sea. Neither of the birds seemed to notice Lupé at this point, and he suggested, "Maybe we better tell her the tuna story again."

"That one's totally dry. Besides, no matter what we say, she'll know we were sealing."

"But not that we got dipped!"

"And a flighteous dip it was!" the sister agreed.

Laughing, they brushed wings. Then they noticed Lupé hovering overhead. The two birds popped into the air and, in unison, said, "Sorry, bird." The sister added, "Didn't mean to flip you." Having said their apology, they were off again, flying like terns in a tornado.

Lupé had a pretty good idea where they were headed. He got a bearing on their direction, which was no easy task, and followed along behind the wild pair.

Up ahead, beyond the truant twins, Lupé saw a formation of petrels approaching, led by a very capable flier. That must be the instructor, he guessed. The strongest bird always flies first so that he or she can split the wind for those who follow. It is a position of honor for the bird and a sign of respect for the wind.

Ten youngsters trailed behind the instructor, the smallest of which was just a peck of a bird. Lupé watched the sister and brother approach. The group stopped, and the lead bird flew off with the two. When the three returned, the brother and sister were flying straighter and tighter than Lupé had ever seen. The group broke off into pairs. Lupé saw that Tapao was not among them. As he glided closer, he wondered whether the instructor would be more like Tapao or Bog. It was time to find out.

Lupé flew up behind the one who was obviously in charge, the lone adult. The youngsters paid little attention to his arrival. They were busy with their latest assignment, running on the surface of the sea. This teacher seemed to start with the basics, and Lupé liked that.

What happened next caught Lupé slightly by surprise. The instructor turned around to face him. She was a female. Lupé had taken for granted that he would find a male. He tried to hide his surprise and asked himself why he had made such an assumption. At the same time, he explained who he was and why Tapao had sent him.

The instructor, whose name was Sirka, listened courteously, even though Tapao had not informed her about inviting Lupé to visit her group. Before he was through with his introduction, Lupé apologized at his apparent surprise at finding a female instructor. He explained that he had never seen a gathering like this before, that anytime he saw youngsters being taught to fish, it was done by a male, usually a relative.

Sirka was not pleased with Lupé's comments, although she did respect his candor. It was obviously not the first time someone had drawn a distinction between her gender and her position. Sirka calmly said, "There are three reasons why I am here. The first is that I believe it's important for the young to learn how to feed themselves. Secondly, I happen to be the best fisher-bird in the flock. And lastly, this is not a duty others are screeching to get."

"Why is that?" Lupé asked. "Most flocks and families hold the teaching of their young in the highest light."

"So did mine," Sirka added.

"Well, when did they stop thinking that way?"

"When the flock's best fisher-bird became a female." Sirka continued, "Actually, Tapao and many others believe in what I'm doing, but there are those who don't."

"Let me take a wild guess," Lupé said rhetorically. "Could Bog be one of them?" He neither needed nor received an answer.

The more he thought about it, the more Lupé liked the idea of a female instructor. "Why not?" he asked himself. The petrel looked forward to seeing just how good the Darum's best fisher-bird really was.

Sirka turned to the youngsters and said one word. "Plunge."

The smaller petrels climbed into the sky and paused, and then an avalanche of tiny birds rained on the sea. As soon as they struck the water, they darted back into the sky and plunged again.

While the students were busy with their latest exercise, Sirka spoke with Lupé. Rather than explain when he would address the group, Sirka politely suggested that maybe it wasn't such a good idea for Lupé to speak at all.

She said, "Students need someone they can depend on. Anyone can fly in here, say a few words, and leave. What these youngsters need is someone to work with them, to be here for them."

"Well, all Tapao asked . . ." Lupé defended.

"I know, I know. I appreciate your coming out here. And please don't think that I'm asking you to work with us on a regular basis. Actually, that brings me to my other reason."

"You have *another* reason why it's not a good idea for me to be here?" Lupé couldn't believe what he was hearing.

"I don't think it's such a good idea for you to speak to the group, because, well . . . Do you really think you have the skills?"

"The *what*?!" Lupé was screechless.

"I just get the feeling," Sirka continued, "that maybe your flock doesn't know as much about fishing as the Darums. Honestly, the last time I saw you, you couldn't even stand up."

Then Lupé realized . . . she was the one at the shore. No wonder she thought he was such a clam. It relieved Lupé to know he was far enough from shore that Stithl couldn't possibly see or hear what was going on. Sirka noticed a student who concerned her, and she flew off. The young petrel was catching fish but dropping them in the sea. Most were dead or injured when he released them. Sirka flew at him and deflected his dive before he could take another fish from the ocean.

She hovered over the water with him and said, "We fish for one reason. If you're not going to eat it, don't kill it." The instructor was firm but gentle. Her student understood, and so did Lupé. Like Tapao, Sirka flew the good flight.

Since she had cast aspersions on the fishing prowess of the Gwattas, Lupé felt he had something to prove to Sirka. Looking around, he noticed that several of the younger birds were getting wobbly from hitting the water with their heads. Lupé could see that they really didn't have the strength yet for the technique they were practicing, so he gathered them together and showed them another.

The petrels listened as Lupé said, "I bet you're feeling a little dizzy right about now." The youngsters nodded their spinning little heads. "Then let me show you a way to fish that's a lot of fun . . . and a lot less painful."

One brave student peeped, "But all of the fish have gone."

"Well," Lupé answered, "when it comes to fish, the currents may think they are in control, but a little skill can make a big difference. So if you do this right, your head won't hurt, and the fish might just come back."

The young ones became very interested. They realized they were about to learn something the older students didn't know, something maybe even Sirka didn't know.

"This is a technique I learned from the Skimmers. So what do you think it's called?"

There was a pause, a silence. Tiny brains were hard at work. Then a shaky voice peeped, "Skimming?"

"Good!" Lupé enthused. He hadn't noticed, but Sirka watched from a safe distance. Behind her, the rest of the class also looked on.

"Have any of you seen a skimmer before?" Little heads with petite beaks shook from side to side, signaling they had not.

"A skimmer is just about my size. It's white with black trim, but the most fascinating thing about the skimmer is its big orange-and-black beak. The lower half is much larger and longer than the upper half, so they do this technique a bit better than we will, but that doesn't mean it can't work for you."

Lupé lined the birds up wing to wing. He flew with them back and forth across a small, flat patch of sea. After each pass, he told them to fly a flap lower until they got as low as they could without actually touching the water. The youngsters were already very good on the wing. They mastered this skill easily, and Lupé praised them lavishly.

"How low can you go?" he dared.

Next, he challenged them to fly as they had been doing, but he told the birds to drag their beaks in and out of the water. After a few passes and a couple dipped petrels, they mastered the timing of the task.

Finally, Lupé told them to do just what they had been doing, but to open their beaks this time, slipping only the lower half into the sea. For the first few passes, the little ones gagged on the water that streamed into their throats. Eventually, they got the hang of it. When the small group could fly across the water, running their beaks along the surface without stumbling or choking, Lupé explained the skimmers' method.

"Are any of you wondering what we're doing?" he asked.

"I am," Sirka spoke. She grinned and came closer, the others following behind her. Lupé's audience was larger than he had thought.

One of the little ones said, "We've worked very hard, but we haven't caught any fish. And I'm getting hungry."

"Well, now that you're an expert skimmer, let's fish," Lupé replied. He darted across the calm sea, slicing his closed beak through the water. A silvery line trailed behind him where the sun caught the crease in the sea. Lupé turned sharply and retraced the fading line with an open beak. In an instant, he snapped it shut and popped into the air. He returned to the youngsters and dropped something into the open mouth of the hungry student.

The little petrel swallowed. "It works," he declared. "It's a fish!"

With that, Lupé's little group raced belly feathers above the sea, dragging their beaks through the water. Before they completed one pass, the older ones joined in. Soon, everyone was catching fish like skimmers. One of the youngsters, who had a slight overbeak, had some trouble until he angled his head sideways. With the larger half of his beak in the water, he skimmed out more fish than any of the others. Lupé was astounded how skillfully the youngster and his classmates flew.

While all this was going on, Tapao quietly drifted in. He floated off to one side and sat on the water unnoticed, observing the scene.

Several youngsters who were having difficulty asked Lupé to demonstrate once more. He looked to Sirka for approval. She waved him on and then joined the small group, saying, "You didn't ask my permission the first time. Why start now?"

Lupé performed the technique just as he had previously. Well, maybe this time he did it with a little more flair than was needed. Obviously impressed with himself, Lupé glided past the group with a large silver fish hanging across his beak.

With fish in mouth, he mumbled a proclamation. "The skimmers say, 'A frish in the break is worf trwo in the srurf.'"

The instant Lupé said the word "srurf," Sirka shot up from the sea and bit Lupé's tail. He was so stunned that the fish slipped from his mouth and fell toward the green water. But before it struck, Sirka cut underneath and snatched the treat for herself. She splashed down in front of the group and said, "Now tell Lupé what the Darums say."

In unison—Tapao included—they recited, "A fish in the *belly* is worth two in the *beak*."

Petrels have a phrase for what Sirka did to Lupé. They called it "having your beak cleaned." It was something youngsters would do to each other all the time. It was also something any mature petrel should have been able to avoid. Worse than the embarrassment, Sirka had taken the fish just as the taste teased Lupé's tongue. He was left with nothing but an empty sensation in his belly, juices flowing with nothing to digest.

That was the worst of it, but as Lupé usually found the case to be, there was also a good side. It had been a long time since he had had his beak cleaned. It signaled that Lupé was back among petrels—among friends, he hoped.

Lupé nodded humbly. He was thankful that others could not see the crimson flesh beneath his feathers. "Now *I* have learned," he said with metaphorical egg on his face.

When everyone was done laughing at Lupé, the youngsters returned to skimming. Having seen the technique demonstrated, Sirka could now perform it flawlessly as she helped those who could not.

The two petrels that had crashed into Lupé earlier in the day approached him. The female said, "Hi. We just wanted to tell you that we weren't sealing around before because we're major squids or anything. We just love flying so much, we get into trouble sometimes." The brother nodded enthusiastically as his sister spoke.

Lupé could see that the two birds loved to fly. Not even their thick plumage could hide their massive chest and wing muscles, the type of muscles that only come from being constantly in the air. "The part about loving to fly makes a lot of sense to me," Lupé said, "but I'm not sure I see the connection from that to getting into trouble."

The two birds looked at Lupé as though he couldn't see the ocean beneath him.

Then the brother asked, "Well, now that we've explained ourselves, would you be so glide as to aid us with that completely current skimming thing?"

A request like that, Lupé could not refuse, partly because he wasn't quite sure what it meant. He was ready to fly off with the two petrels when he noticed Tapao and Sirka talking. The flock's leader called him over.

Tapao began by asking Lupé if he would be interested in working with the group whenever he could find the time. The leader pointed out that even though they weren't as bad off as the Gwattas, the Darums' numbers had fallen. Tapao was genuinely concerned.

Lupé, however, directed his response to Sirka. He wanted to know how she felt.

"If you don't want to come on a regular basis, you would still be welcome to drop in on us. It's okay with me," Sirka said, somewhat unenthusiastically. She looked at the skimming frenzy, smiled, and added, "They seem to like you."

"But do you?" Lupé asked.

Sirka clenched her beak like she had swallowed a rancid clam, nodded her head three times, and said, "I think so."

Lupé looked at the two petrels facing him. He found himself promising, "As long as I am on these islands, I will make time for the youngsters."

Tapao seemed pleased. Sirka seemed surprised. She said, "Lupé, you seem to be a nice enough petrel, but I don't really know you, so I think I should speak my mind in front of both you and Tapao. I don't want to see some competitive thing come up between us."

"Like cleaning one's beak?" the cleanee asked the cleaner.

Sirka acknowledged the point and continued, "I just don't want any male-female competition to get in the way of what we do here. It's important to me because it's important to them. They will mimic what they see us do."

Lupé thought for a moment. He tried to put himself in Sirka's feathers. After all, this was really her domain. He was the outsider—the invader. So Lupé said, "You couldn't be more right. It seems to me there's really only one way to do this. It's *your* group. I'll help however I can, however you want me to."

Sirka turned to Tapao and said, "It's okay with me. I think Lupé will help us a great deal."

"Then it's done," Tapao declared.

Lupé shrugged his wings and nodded. Part of him felt good to be involved with a flock of petrels, and part of him wondered if it might be wiser to stay away.

The petrel's thought was broken when Tapao asked Lupé to return to Galahope with him. The leader explained right away that he wanted Lupé to meet with Bog. Tapao hoped the two birds could be friends, and he thought another meeting might help. Lupé wasn't so sure, but he flew along anyway.

On the flight back, Lupé tried to decide how he felt about what was happening to him. He had conflicting emotions. He had to admit to himself that he felt comfortable and that he was as happy as he'd been in a long time. It was nice to be with petrels, but they really weren't his flock. So Lupé couldn't help wondering whether it would be wise to leave, to keep searching for his own kind. But if he really believed that Galahope and the Islands of Life were the same, then he must be where Pettr wanted him to be.

As if all this wasn't confusing enough, another thought took flight. Many pairs of birds arrived at their nesting sites at approximately the same time, even though each individual might come from a very different place. Maybe this was where Pettr wanted Lupé to wait to be sent a mate. And as long as he was here waiting, Lupé saw no reason why he should not help the Darums. If he ever did start a Gwatta flock on these islands, he might need their help. Lupé had a strange feeling that the nest he had just built could be the home for the future of his flock.

Until Pettr led him differently, he would trust the voice within, wait here, and continue to pray for the answer, whatever it might be. If he just kept flying the good flight, Lupé believed Pettr would provide.

Floating down from above, Lupé and Tapao descended on the island. Bog had likely been alerted to their arrival, because he and several others waited on a boulder just beyond the reach of the surf. When he could see for himself who it was that flew with Tapao, Bog became visibly upset. Just as fog or clouds can remove the sun from the afternoon sky, hate steamed up and covered any traces of understanding that Bog might have. He became as cold and hard as the rock he perched on.

Tapao landed on the same boulder as Bog. When the leader touched down, all but Bog left the rock. Lupé placed himself next to Tapao, across from Bog. He knew which bird he'd have to watch.

Bog did not hesitate or preamble with pleasantries. "I don't want him here."

"*You* don't?" Tapao asked.

"He will be trouble. He does not belong and never will."

"Why doesn't he belong?" the leader questioned.

Lupé kept his beak shut. No one had to tell him to clam up.

"I don't want him here," Bog bellowed, "because there's not enough food, nesting sites . . . or females."

When Lupé heard that, he couldn't help but sputter. Tapao also grinned, but Bog didn't. He was serious. That laugh and that smile were only two more reasons for him to hate the outsider.

Lupé stared at the crooked, battle-chipped beak across from him. While the two Darums continued disagreeing, Lupé imagined what type of scar Bog's beak would leave on a victim, but his attention returned to the discussion at wing when he heard . . .

"We don't need him. What can he do for us other than cause trouble? And mark my words, he will be trouble."

"I'm sure you'll do your best to see that he is," Tapao responded. Then he told Bog, "Lupé will teach the young with Sirka. He is to be treated as one of the flock."

"I should have guessed," Bog sneered. "He belongs with those hatchlings and that female."

Now it was time for Lupé to speak. It really wasn't, but the petrel couldn't stand by and listen to Bog any longer. He also didn't want Bog to think this "outsider" was weak or afraid, so he said, "The *female* I saw today could teach you a few things about feeding and flying."

Bog seemed stunned. He turned to Lupé. Rage poured from his eyes, soaked his dark feathers, and dripped all around him.

Lupé, occasionally one to take things a flap too far, continued, "But then again, you're probably not ready for Sirka yet. You'd probably learn more from the hatchlings at this point."

Lupé became silent when Tapao cast him a disappointed look. It was not the reaction Lupé hoped his outburst would elicit.

The petrel changed his tone, "I only want to do what I can for the young, to help them become proud petrels."

"Proud petrels like you, I suppose," Bog shot back with disdain. "Why do you want to help us? Why is it important to you? And what would you know about petrels? Look at you."

Lupé remained composed. "Certainly, I look more like a petrel than a pigeon." Bog did not know what a pigeon was, so he did not like the sound of this at all. "Don't I look more like a petrel than any bird you've ever seen?"

Bog proved there were no limits to how narrow minded he could be by saying, "I look like a petrel. Tapao looks like a petrel." And pointing to all the others, he continued, "They look like petrels. But I don't know what you are, with that pale plumage, that split tail, not to mention that man-flock ring around your leg. Tapao, he is a disease, and he will infect our flock."

"I haven't really seen you add to it," the leader sniped.

"I'd be happy to . . . if you'd give me your niece's wing."

Ah, Lupé thought, *so Tapao has a niece. Where has he been hiding her?*

"Bog, we both know that's her decision, and we both know how she would respond. There are other females."

Whether Bog actually loved Tapao's niece or not, nobody knew. But it was obvious that he did not want to see another male marry the leader's only living relative.

Now Lupé was getting even more interested. It seemed to him that there was more going on between Tapao and Bog than a debate about an outsider.

Although it was about as practical as trying to hatch a rock, Lupé decided to try reasoning with the hostile Darum one more time. "Bog," he said, "why is different automatically bad? I am not an accident. Pettr has breathed life into both of us."

"Pettr doesn't know who or what you are."

Lupé wanted to ask Bog how he could say what Pettr knew, but after seeing how useless his appeal was, the petrel merely said, "Don't be so sure Pettr wouldn't recognize me."

Bog grew tired of all the talk. With finality and venom, he said, "I do not like him, and I do not want him here."

"And that has been my point all along," Tapao interrupted. "You simply do not like Lupé. Well, I do."

"He is not part of my flock."

"If you ever lead a flock, that might mean something, but for now, you'll do as I say."

Bog had turned to leave before Tapao finished the sentence, so the leader was talking to the back of his head. Bog tossed a blast of hot oil at Lupé's feet and directed a comment just loud enough for the others to hear at Tapao, "For now, old bird . . . for now."

Those who had gathered on the surrounding rocks and shrubs followed Bog as he left. Some laughed, others flew off silently. After they had gone, Tapao said, "All the hate in the world is inside each of us, and so is all the love . . . Each bird must choose what to give others. It seems Bog has made his choice."

Lupé wondered if Tapao was issuing some type of threat or if his words did not reach that far.

"Looks like the meeting wasn't such a good idea after all," Lupé observed.

"Nonsense. We have an understanding. Each of us knows how the other feels. It may not be much, but it is something. And like all storms, this will blow over."

"Do you still think I should work with the youngsters?" Lupé asked.

"Of course. Sirka could use the help, and the young ones like you. What Bog thinks is not important. Besides, he had an opportunity to teach the young and chose to waste his time doing other things. And as far as Bog's issues with finding a mate, if he wants a future with my niece, the final decision rests with her. She is the one who must approve."

Ah, Lupé thought. *Perhaps Tapao shares command of the flock with his niece. There might be another who holds power here. Maybe Tapao remains as leader only because he and his niece together are stronger than Bog alone.*

Lupé smiled and declared, "Then it's time you introduced me to your niece!"

The petrel was shocked to hear Tapao say, "You know where Sirka is, but I can save you . . ." The rest of the words slid off Lupé like water rolling down his oily feathers. Tapao finished his statement, nodded, and flew off, leaving Lupé on the barren boulder to gather his thoughts.

"So, Sirka is Tapao's niece," he said to himself. "I'm always the last to pluck stuff like that."

When Lupé returned to his nest, he found Stithl crunching a rather large green leaf in his mouth.

"Stithl," Lupé inquired, "do you know anything about a female Darum named Sirka?"

The lizard swallowed the leaf. "Oh, ya know `er name. I wundert how long id't dagke."

"You mean you knew who she was and you didn't tell me?"

"I know everyone on dis islant, bud ya neva agsk't . . . An, if memry serves me, when ya med her down ad da shore, didn'd ya say dad ya weren'd inderesdet, dad ya only wandet da help'er metidate?"

"Please, Stithl, let's not start that again. The situation has changed."

"I'll bed id has," Stithl said with a reptilian grin.

"Well, now I'm asking. What else do you know about her?"

"Whudda *you* know?"

"I know that she's Tapao's niece. She works with the young. And I guess she has some history with Bog."

"Ya know all dad?"

"Yes, I do."

The iguana nodded as though he were very impressed with Lupé's knowledge. "Den ya don'd know nuddin'." It was tough to see whether Stithl enjoyed frustrating Lupé or not, but it was easy to see that he was good at it.

Just to make Lupé squirm a little more, Stithl took his time responding. When the petrel's patience seemed thoroughly exhausted, Stithl told him what he knew. The lizard said it was true that Sirka was the premier fisher-bird of the Darums, and hence one of the flock's best fliers, possibly its best. He claimed she was incredibly independent, saying, "Sirgka does whud Sirgka wands." Because of that, many in the flock disapproved of her.

Stithl felt that Bog saw her as a way to increase his status among the Darums, so he perpetuated the idea that there was something between them. The other males were either too jealous of her skill or too afraid of Bog to approach her. And not even Sirka liked the idea of fighting Bog. Also, many of the females did not like the way Sirka ignored certain ideas regarding how a proper petrel should behave. But Stithl was quick to point out that there were those devoted to Sirka, mostly the young and some of their parents.

No matter how any of the Darum petrels felt, there was no denying that Sirka was their leader's niece. The iguana stressed that even at his advanced age, Tapao was still the best friend, and consequently the worst enemy, any bird in the flock could have. Lupé was happy to hear that, since he considered himself Tapao's friend.

Stithl summed up his profile by saying, "Lizartly, I dingk she's a lovely creadcha."

"How do you feel about Bog?" Lupé asked.

"He's nod so lovely a creadcha. Bog's a droublet birt who don'd know his beagk from his budd aboud anydin'. From da negk up, he's nuddin' bud empdy feddas. All'e eva does is walgk up'n down da shoreline fillin' his belly wid jellyfish, grabs, an glams."

"But that's what you do, Stithl."

"I'm suppose'da do dad! I'm a lizart, ya scallob! Don'd inderrubd me. An Bog's frients `r as gruel an gonfus't as he is, `cepd dey're stupit'r, gause dey do whudeva he says."

"Why do you think Bog doesn't fish?"

"I guess id dagkes doo mugch effit. Or maybe he's afrait he don'd do id as well as Sirgka. Ya know, she hades `im, bud don'd dell `er I dolt ya."

"You really know her that well?"

"Woot I be able da dell ya all dis juicy sduff if I didn'd?"

Lupé didn't know whether Stithl was telling the truth or not. It was so difficult to tell with an iguana, especially this one.

The two chatted on as the sun faded from the sky. When it became dark, Lupé escorted the lizard back to his rock. It wasn't very far away.

He froze when he saw it. His heart stopped, and his stomach emptied. Stithl not only didn't see it, he stood in it! Lupé shoved him aside. In front of them was a large footprint. The man-flock was on the island.

Stithl hissed, "Lubé, whudd'a ya doin'? Why't ya shove me?"

"Quiet," his friend replied. "Don't you see the footprint? The man-flock is here."

"A'gourse he is," Stithl said. He walked back to the footprint and sat down in it. Lupé was repulsed and confused, but even more so when he heard Stith's next comment.

"An if da one who mate dis was stantin' in id, I't walgk righd up da `im an give `im a nice big hug."

Lupé could not believe what he heard. The lizard had seemed so sane . . . well, almost sane. All the petrel could say was, "Stithl?" as if suddenly there was a different iguana standing in front of him.

"Dey may nod've ton righd by you, Lupé, bud if da resd'a ligke da dwo dad I know . . . I love man."

This was beyond the petrel's comprehension.

"Dere'r dwo of `em," Stithl said. "A male an a female, I guess. Dey live bassd da brushwood, bagck in da bines. Dey wuh oud here dotay while ya wuh gone wid Dabao."

Oud here dotay . . . The words spun like a tsunami in Lupé's mind. He thought for a moment and then told Stithl, "If the man-flock is here, I must go. These cannot be the Islands of Life."

"Ya don'd have da go anywhere. Dese dwo won'd hurd ya, I'm delling ya."

"But they are the man-flock." It was Lupé's only response, as though it was all he had to say.

"Drusd me," Stithl continued. "I've wadch't `em my whole life, an I've neva seen `em harm any lizart or birt. Now, if ya were a rad, I't dell ya da worry."

"They don't like rats?"

"Dey hade rads. As'a madda a fagcd, dey kill `em."

Lupé liked what he heard but couldn't accept it. He believed Stithl had to be mistaken.

The iguana sensed his companion's doubts and said, "Gum on, I'll show ya."

As he followed Stithl into the bush, the petrel remembered the first thing Kurah had ever told him about the man-flock. His father had said, "You stay away from the hungry hawk because you know what to expect from him. With the man-flock, there's no telling. They can be kind, and they can be brutal. We must protect ourselves, so you must assume the worst . . . avoid them." It was advice Lupé lived by.

"Pssst . . . Pssst . . . Pssst . . ." Finally, Stithl caught the bird's attention. The lizard found what he was looking for. They were standing in the midst of the thorny bracken that separated Lupé's nest from the colony. Under a bush lay what looked like a large pair of open jaws, but they were not contained inside any type of head. They were just there on the soil, open and poised to close.

Lupé had never seen anything like it before. It looked dangerous, so he did not advance. Stithl, however, had seen plenty of these. He called them "black jaws." The iguana explained that the man-flock baited and opened the jaws and that their bite was fatal.

"Dey'r jaws widoud eyes," he warned. But the bait the man-flock used didn't appeal to any of Galahope's residents other than rodents. So if Lupé was careful not to stumble into them, the jaws could actually serve him. Those who left the footprints collected the dead rodents every day. Stithl assumed they liked the taste of rat, but whatever the reason, he and the other creatures were grateful to have the rodents controlled.

Listening to Stithl, Lupé was reminded of Gilgongo's story. Twice now, he had heard of the man-flock protecting other creatures. To the petrel, however, it did not make sense. It was not the man-flock he knew.

Since the lizard had pointed one out, Lupé noticed several more pairs of the black jaws as he returned to his nest. One set was barely a flap from his home. It made Lupé nervous, but he knew where they were, and hoped that they might protect him someday, so Lupé didn't try to move them. The thing that upset the petrel the most was the idea that the man-flock would pass so close to his nest when they checked the jaws. Stithl might feel they could be trusted, but he was never taken by them. Lupé also worried that the baited jaws might actually attract rats to this part of the island.

After a restless sleep, the petrel woke to a strange sight. From where he nested under the sheltering shrub, he could see that the jaws had claimed a victim during the night. A rat was tangled between the tight teeth. The rodent did not move. It looked as though he was sleeping, and Lupé would have thought so except for one thing. The creature's neck had been replaced by the cold, closed jaws. The tiny piece of meat that had attracted the rat still hung from the scavenger's jaws, just as it hung from the larger jaws.

The petrel rose to investigate but stopped when he heard a noise that made his feathers tense. Gradually, the sound grew louder. It was the slow, rhythmic gait of the man-flock. Lupé knew what was happening, and he didn't like it. His first instinct was to fly, but it was too late. The rare petrel did not want to be seen. He backed deeper into his nest, afraid to even breathe.

Two large feet, each one big enough to crush Lupé, stepped up to the jaws. A hand reached down. The blood and bone were wiped away, and the jaws were spread open. A fresh piece of meat was put into place, inviting another visit from a reckless rodent.

The hands reached down again. This time, they picked up the carcass of the dead rat. The head hung from the body, attached by a shredded sliver of skin. Then the feet pivoted and stepped toward Lupé. "Have I been seen?" the petrel wondered as he backed still deeper into the bush.

Crash, crush, snap. The feet came closer and closer until they were next to the nest. Something fell, but the feet kept moving. Soon they were gone.

The petrel emerged slowly. He was in no rush to greet danger. When he finally felt confident, he searched for what had fallen. It was easy to locate. The rodent's head had snapped free from its body and rested in some dry weeds a few steps from Lupé's nest.

Lupé examined the head. It did not bother him, especially considering it was a head that might have attacked him during the night. The lifelessness and the death, however, reminded him of Barau. Thoughts of his younger brother were interrupted when a petrel from the colony landed nearby. It looked like one Lupé had seen with Bog, the one called Wohat. The visitor seemed to be alone, and Lupé wondered what Bog's right-wing bird might want with him. He stepped into the open to find out.

Wohat warned Lupé that if he stayed near the Darums any longer, there would be trouble. He said that Bog did not fear Tapao and Bog could force Lupé to leave if he decided to.

Once again, Lupé explained that he meant no trouble, but he would not be forced out. He told Wohat that he did not fear Bog or any other.

Lupé meant what he said. If Pettr wanted him on this island, he would fight for the right to stay.

Wohat froze. He lifted a wing and motioned Lupé not to move, not to speak. Something terrified the Darum. He lowered his beak and peered into the brush. Lupé could not see what was there, but he had a good idea what it might be. He stepped closer to the visitor and saw the rodent's head poking through the grass with a lifeless grin.

Lupé found it interesting that Wohat had chosen to warn him. The Darum could just as easily have flown away without saying anything. *There might be hope*, Lupé thought. Then he said, "He's dead."

Wohat inhaled. He smelled the death, looked back to Lupé, and approached the head. He pecked at it and stepped away. He pecked again, then dragged the head into the sunlight.

"I told you he was dead," Lupé said.

For some reason, Wohat looked very frightened. He asked, "Did you do this?"

The Darum did not consider the black jaws. Clearly, Bog's right-wing bird was as dim as the rest of his followers. Lupé seized the opportunity to have some fun and to perhaps plant a little fear into Bog's circle.

Wohat timidly repeated, "Did you do this?"

Lupé nodded and said, "Yes, the rodent left me no choice."

"But how?" The puzzled, fearful words slipped from Wohat's beak.

"My flock does not like to kill . . . but we are very capable." Lupé paused while the sight of the rodent's severed head worked itself deep into Wohat's memory.

The messenger asked, "Where is the body?"

Lupé hoped he would ask that. He grinned and said, "I eat rats." Then he forced himself to belch, grinned again, and asked, "Would you care to share the rest of the head with me? Don't worry, there's plenty for both of us. You can even take some back to your burrow."

Wohat didn't speak. He just stood there with his beak hanging open.

Finally, Lupé asked, "Is there anything else you wish to caution me about on Bog's behalf?" By the time the rat-eater completed the question, Bog's messenger was in the air, heading toward the colony. Stithl strode out from behind a rock, smiled, and said, "Lube', I godda atmid, I ligke ya style."

Time passed, and the petrel continued to pray for the special female who never arrived. Little changed. Bog maintained his hostility but did nothing to act on it, probably because Lupé and Tapao had grown very fond of each other, and possibly because the rumor of Lupé's strange taste for rodent was still fresh in Bog's mind.

Usually one to turn the other beak, Lupé believed in giving unpleasantness every opportunity to pass. Battling Bog did not appeal to him. It was not the type of fight he believed in. It really had nothing to do with survival and thus was senseless. So he ignored the threats and taunts that came from Bog and his followers. Lupé continued as he had since his arrival—he avoided confrontations. It was a decision that seemed to please Tapao.

Out at sea, Lupé and Sirka kept working with the young, who were getting bigger every day, as was the group. Ideas and methods were catching on. More and more young petrels flew out to learn what they could. Now, instead of a dozen students, Sirka and Lupé had more than twenty. At times, it was birdensome, but they did the best they could. Sirka and Lupé would not refuse any bird who wanted to learn.

Some in the colony talked about splitting the group into early and late sessions, but the instructors decided against it. They liked the chemistry that had developed between them. Tapao, who often took part in the sessions at sea, agreed with their decision. However, the fishing lessons did change in one respect.

Lupé and Sirka were the kind of petrels who got along with all types of birds. When they saw how well the skimmers' technique worked, they began inviting guest speakers. Pelicans, gulls, boobies, flightless cormorants, gannets, terns, penguins, and whoever happened by the islands—all explained and demonstrated how they fed. Even Stithl gave a lesson on shoreline scavenging. The youngsters learned a great deal. They became very skilled . . . and Bog became very angry.

By now, Lupé was well acquainted with the brother and sister who had flown into him that first day at sea. Their names were Yip and Kelp. They were, without question, the best fliers in the class, so Lupé often used them as assistants.

Most of the group's newer members already had an understanding of the basics. Even though many still tripped over swells when walking on water and some would allow fish to squirm from their beaks before swallowing, Sirka and Lupé tended to stress group skills over individual accomplishments.

Flock-work, they believed, was more a philosophy than a skill. It called for birds to work together to feed each other. They had to anticipate problems and needed to be concerned at all times for those who flew with them. If they cooperated, assumed roles, were patient, and sacrificed, all would eat, and they would eat better than if they fed alone.

In order to illustrate the notion, Sirka, Lupé, Yip, and Kelp searched for schools of fish. When one of them located a school, the other three would descend on it. Each would take a turn tracking the fish from above so that the others would not lose the moving meal.

The four petrels were very successful. The youngsters enjoyed the display. They bobbed up and down as they sat on the water watching. Lupé could see that the young birds were itching to join the feast.

Occasionally, Yip became so involved with his own feeding, he forgot to help the others. Whenever this happened, the petrels would have to stop and search for the school again, but Yip's selfishness did accomplish something. It showed the youngsters how quickly and how completely things fall apart when one forgets his flock-mates.

Whenever Yip floated off to feed himself, Sirka and Lupé refrained from scolding him. Instead, one of the instructors or Kelp would fly by and clean Yip's beak before he could enjoy a meal gathered at the expense of his companions.

After a thorough beak cleaning, Sirka quietly reminded her student, "You have left the nest and are part of a flock. That means others are tied to you. Take care of them as you would yourself. They will do the same for you. You will make each other stronger."

When the rest of the group tried flock-work, there was no shortage of problems. Some of the spotters flew so low, they couldn't see the entire school and would lose the little fish. Then they would overreact and fly so high, their companions couldn't hear the directions the spotter squawked, and the flock would lose the school again. But when the youngsters finally caught on and remembered to relieve the spotter, the petrels had an enormous feast. The group flew back to Galahope bloated, proud, and a little lower in the sky than usual.

During the time that Lupé spent with the Darums, he and Tapao became more than friends. In a sense, Tapao had become a surrogate uncle for Lupé, offering advice, company, and hope. The Darum leader was an old bird with a young attitude, who faced problems with the knowledge of experience and the enthusiasm of youth. Tapao's mind had not faded with age. If anything, it had become sharper, clearer, and closer to the truth.

The colony's leader returned Lupé's affection. He was happy the Gwatta was among them. Tapao understood that Lupé had already seen more in his life than most birds ever would. The leader loved hearing stories about Lupé's encounters with the man-flock and other creatures. Tapao was also impressed with Lupé's devotion to Pettr. He was convinced that Lupé would one day become a savn, something no Darum had ever achieved. *This is a bird*, he thought, *that Pettr has touched.* And so, Tapao finally decided to tell Lupé what he knew of Pakeet.

"I knew your grandmother," he said once again.

Although it was something he had been waiting to hear, the comment caught Lupé by surprise. He listened intently and said nothing that might interrupt or silence Tapao.

"It was long ago, when our flock was larger and I was younger. We lived on the Islands of Black Sand to the northwest. She looked like you—paler than us, with a split tail.

"Pakeet was a tough bird to figure out. On the one wing, she loved to have fun. She could have a good time doing almost anything, simple things, stuff that would bore most of us. But on the other wing, your grandmother was the prayingest bird I ever saw. She could become very serious without any warning. She was already a savn when I met her, the youngest I'd ever seen.

"Her spirituality is what I remember most about her. She really seemed to be in touch with Pettr. Sometimes, I felt I could actually see him in her. He lived inside her soul. And so, no matter what she did, Pettr was there. It was strange and wonderful. Even now, when I think of her, I don't just see her, I feel her. She didn't just meet you, she gave some of herself to you. A little piece of Pakeet, even now, lives on in me . . ."

"And in me too," Lupé agreed.

"We seemed to fly into each other a great deal, on the open sea, on the Islands of Black Sand, and also where your flock nested on Gwatta."

The sound of his birthplace, hearing the actual word spoken by another, flushed and warmed Lupé. It had been a long time since someone else had casually said, "Gwatta." It felt good. Hearing the word reminded Lupé that his home was real, that his flock was real. But it also made him sad to think that Gwatta and its lives were in the past. The island flock he knew was gone.

Tapao continued talking. He had no idea Lupé's mind had flown from the conversation. ". . . and when we were forced from the Black Sand to Galahope, I never saw her again."

"She was wonderful, wasn't she," Lupé declared more than asked.

Tapao acknowledged his younger friend and nodded his head in agreement. He was not merely appeasing Lupé. The Darum knew Pakeet, and he missed her too.

Then Lupé felt a strange sensation. Something inside told him there was more to Tapao's story. After all, why would Tapao wait to tell him this? He was keeping something from Lupé.

"You really never saw my grandmother after you left the Black Sand?"

Tapao did not answer. He seemed to be working something out in his mind. Maybe he was listening to the same inner voice that guided Lupé. Finally, he replied, "I did not see her in the sense you mean."

"Then how did you see her?"

Again, Tapao hesitated. He wanted to choose his words carefully. "I did see her once more. Pakeet came to me when we first arrived here. She came to me at night, in a dream, but she was very real. We spoke and played, just as we did when we were younger. And before she left—before I woke—she told me that I would meet her grandson one day. He would come to Galahope, and he would need my help. That was the last time I saw Pakeet. And now you are here, just as she prophesied you would be."

"And you are giving me your help, just as she asked."

"We are helping each other."

Lupé wondered how his grandmother could possibly have known what would happen. And if she did, she must also have known about his capture. Why hadn't she warned him in his youth? He asked Tapao, "Did she tell you anything else?" Lupé hoped some clue, some answer was left with his friend.

But the leader said that he had shared everything, and this time the grandson believed him.

Then, as if he had read the petrel's mind, Tapao said, "She spoke nothing of a female, nothing about whether a female Gwatta might come to you or where you might search."

Lupé knew he would be spending a lot of time praying and meditating over this conversation. He believed it signaled that something important was going to happen. Lupé reasoned that at the very least, it must mean he was on the right track, since Pakeet's prophesy had been realized.

Stithl wandered out of the green and joined the two birds. That was when the conversation drifted away from Pakeet. Tapoa asked Lupé if there was any truth to the rumor that he ate rats. When the petrel and the iguana finally stopped laughing, Stithl explained what had happened. Tapao also liked Lupé's style. Soon, they were discussing the man-flock and the two who lived on the island. Tapao was very quiet, so Lupé tossed a question his way.

"How do *you* feel about the man-flock? You've never really said anything about them to me."

"I'm happy that they don't bother us here," the Darum said curtly.

But Lupé was not satisfied. "Do you like them as much as Stithl does?"

"I've seen things Stithl has not, and so my opinion comes from another place."

"And what is your opinion?" Lupé pressed.

"I am confused . . . undecided. This egg is not yet hatched. The man-flock is capable of unthinkable extremes, good ones and bad ones. They have so much power. But I think the man-flock's intelligence has not grown at the same rate as their ability. This is only one bird's opinion, but they seem to do things because they are able, not because it is wise or necessary. They are creatures of enormous achievements yet too often have the understanding of seaweed. They are not balanced. Their wings do not work together."

Since Tapao was in such a talkative mood, Stithl asked the petrel what he thought of the butterfly that had helped Lupé escape.

"I am certainly no bird of pray, but it has been explained to me like this. The butterfly is born totally Earth-bound—"

"Like a chick?" Lupé asked.

"Yes, but more so. Eventually, it climbs a tree and hangs from a branch wrapped in itself. The butterfly is defenseless. The creature dies suspended from the branch, rises to the other side, and is born again. It goes back to the same chrysalis that claimed its former life and returns with Pettr's greatest gift, wings. Once it emerges and makes its first flight, the butterfly is able to pass between heaven and Earth at will. It is welcome on either side.

"If it wanted to, the butterfly could live exclusively on the other side. But almost all choose to return to this world, to serve Pettr and his creatures as a link between heaven and Earth. Butterflies do not speak, not only because they lack a mouth, but because they believe nothing says more than actions. They speak through their deeds. The butterfly that came to you, Lupé, was help from the other side, help from Pettr."

It had been quite a night for Lupé. He heard stories about Pakeet and his home and had gained a new perspective on the butterfly that had helped save him from the man-flock.

After Tapao left, Stithl and Lupé went for a walk along the shore. Neither said much. They just enjoyed the evening. It was all they needed to be happy.

Before the petrel reached his nest, he could tell that something had visited while he was gone. It was night, one of those clear quiet evenings lit by a moon not quite full. Lupé scanned the sky. He checked that no clouds could drift by and hide an intruder at the wrong time. He approached cautiously, just in case the visitor was still in the area and turned out to be hostile. *Why would anything be interested in his nest?* Lupé wondered. There were certainly no eggs to steal.

Then the intruder stepped out from under the bush that sheltered Lupé's home. The moonlight poured across the figure, and it hopped back into the darkness. Lupé could tell it was a bird that waited for him, a petrel from the colony. *A friend would not have to hide*, he thought. *Only an enemy would seek the shadows.*

Lupé stood boldly in the bright night. He was prepared to battle for his nesting site. He puffed his feathers, spread his wings, and hissed as he lowered his back to strike. The display was intended to provide a very clear reply to the challenge issued by the petrel who invaded Lupé's nest.

The Gwatta continued his display, hissing and snapping, until finally the trespasser emerged and said, "Lupé, what are you doing?" It was Sirka.

She seemed nervous. She explained that the only reason she had stopped by was to discuss tomorrow's lesson. Lupé didn't believe her. She knew better than to perch on another's nest, even a friend's. And she had never visited to discuss the group before. Actually, she had never seen Lupé outside of teaching the young. Something was wrong. He could tell that there was more to this visit than Sirka had admitted, and he waited for her to get to the truth while she continued her bogus explanation.

Sirka suggested that they stay on the island tomorrow. She wanted to show the youngsters how to find food without using the sea, just in case the Black Death ever touched their waters or the weather prevented them from fishing.

Lupé thought it was a good idea—a lie, but still a good idea. He smiled and said that he would explain to the young males that it was when weather forced petrels to stay in their nests or burrows that the flock's numbers would grow. The two birds shared an innocent giggle over the observation, as they anticipated some of the questions Lupé's comment might elicit.

When they finally stopped sputtering, an awkward silence filled the night. Lupé got the feeling that Sirka would either say goodbye or offer the truth behind her visit. Sirka chose the truth.

When Lupé heard the reason she had come, you could have knocked him over with a strand of hair.

Sirka took a deep breath of cool evening air. She was nervous—very nervous—and used the silence to focus her concentration. She stepped closer to Lupé and looked him in the eyes. They were beak to beak. Only a breath separated them.

Sirka whispered, "It must have been terrible to have your freedom taken."

"There is nothing worse."

"In a sense," Sirka continued, "we are both the same. We are both alone, both waiting."

"You're not alone. You have Tapao, the youngsters, and the Darums. What could you be waiting for?"

"You know what I mean, Lupé."

And for the first time, the petrel thought he understood. But understanding what Sirka meant only confused him more.

Lupé said, "I am alone because I have no choice. I am my flock's orphan. But Sirka, you have chosen to be alone."

Without even blinking, Sirka said, "And now I have made another choice. I choose you, Lupé." Gently, she began to preen the feathers along the nape of Lupé's neck.

His heart began to race as Sirka touched him. It was a sensation he had never felt before. *How could this be happening?* Lupé thought. Sirka was not of his flock. She could not be the one sent by Pettr. All he had to do was leave. But with the moon shining in her eyes, and with Sirka's beak buried in his feathers, Lupé finally admitted something he had known from the moment he first saw her—Sirka was beautiful.

Lupé stepped back from her. He knew he could do only one thing: follow his heart. He cast everything else to the wind and allowed his emotion to speak for him. "I am alone no more," he said. "I have you."

Sirka smiled. "We have each other . . . This is no world to be alone in." She studied Lupé. His black-and-white plumage reminded her of her home, black sand streaked with sliding white foam. It was a powerful memory.

The two birds approached each other again, for the first time. Lupé reached his wing out to Sirka. And then he stopped. He wasn't really sure what to do next. He had never been with a female before. The realization, especially at this moment, made him nervous, frightened. But again, he decided to trust his heart.

They were back in each other's wings. Lupé found himself whispering, "Do you know what I always dreamt of doing?" The two birds looked at each other. Lupé turned to the surf, and Sirka followed him to the quiet *crash-swish*.

Under the moonlight, stroked by the spray of the surf, was where Lupé wanted to find love. The shoreline fizzed and frothed with a fringe of tiny waves. The sea called the pair into the water, and the invitation was readily accepted.

They each spread their wings. Then the breeze joined in, gently lifting them into the air as one. With their union blessed by both wind and sea, Lupé knew it had to be right.

A large cloud was nudged by the wind to reveal a bare moon. In its light, Lupé could see how stunning his mate was. *She is as true as flight on a windless day*, he thought. A steady stream of moisture cascaded down Sirka's sides. Her black feathers had a translucent shine, like sea-soaked lava stone illuminated with starlight. The little drops of water that bounced and dripped off Sirka glistened in the night, sparkling as they fell. Lupé could feel her next to him. She was as soft and warm as white sand in the summer sun. It was a vision, a love he had waited his entire life to find.

Sirka laid her dark head against Lupé's pale breast, snuggling into feathers that looked like they were stolen from gray clouds. Under his plumage, Lupé felt firm and full. *He is striking*, she thought. The pair held each other tightly. Floating in the surf, they began to coo and purr, nuzzle and stroke.

When Lupé and Sirka returned to their nest, Sirka fell asleep. Lupé, however, could not relax. There was too much to think about, too much to sort out. He was amused by the thought of what Stithl would say when he arrived for his daily visit . . . And then Lupé considered how Tapao might react. It is one thing to *like* the outsider, Lupé thought, but when he falls in love with your niece, your only living relative, attitudes could change.

But the more the petrel thought about it, the more he believed Tapao would not be upset with the news. Lupé wondered if this might actually be something Tapao had wanted all along. After all, it was Tapao who had sent him to Sirka in the first place. Was he the one who had designed their future?

Lupé gazed at his mate. Whenever Sirka exhaled, he could feel the air sneaking through his feathers, caressing his skin. Her soothing breath crept past the flesh and climbed inside Lupé, warming his soul and filling something that had been empty too long. Sirka was a blessing. And whatever Tapao or anyone else might think did not matter.

It was done, Lupé reasoned. He had taken a fine mate . . . well, more truthfully, a fine mate had taken him, and he was glad of it. As Lupé sat looking at the stars and listening to the surf, an idea blew into his mind that he could not ignore: offspring. What would they be like? Lupé knew that his children would never be exactly like him, a full-blooded Gwatta. He became disappointed in himself, thinking that he might have traded his flock's purity for his own happiness.

But Lupé knew that even though his offspring might not be pure, some of his flock's heritage and lifestyle would endure. He would see to it. Their young would be neither Gwatta nor Darum, yet they would be both. Lupé wondered if he and Sirka were chosen to create a new flock, which led him to consider something else. All his speculation rested upon one very large assumption: that he and Sirka would even be able to have young together. It was the one thing that would prove whether Lupé's choice was the same as Pettr's.

Just before dawn, as the pair lay next to each other, Lupé woke. Another troubling possibility nagged at him. Now that he and Sirka were nesting, what would he do if a female from his own flock ever turned up? Which would be more important, the obligation to Sirka or the obligation to his flock? From where he sat now, the petrel knew it would be impossible to say. He decided to cross that sea when he came to it.

There was, however, one thing he did know, one thing that would not change. He loved Sirka. And since love was a good thing to build a family on, why not a flock? Lupé accepted that the female who slept next to him was the one sent by Pettr, and he believed that one day, they'd have the young to prove it.

The morning greeted the newlynests with an orange sunrise streaked with yellow and red, dusted by thin, white clouds. It heralded a new life for Lupé and Sirka—theirs. The pair began their first day without words. They stayed close, preened each other, and watched Pettr's eye fill the sky.

When the sun was free from the sea, Sirka prepared to meet her students. She rose, stretched her wings, and ruffled her feathers, hinting that Lupé should also prepare to go. He, however, had a look on his face that Sirka had seen before. She was not surprised when her mate finally asked, "Would you mind if I joined you later? I would like to visit the shore and listen to our world."

Sirka was the type of bird who quickly understood what was said and just as quickly understood what wasn't said. She ran her beak down Lupé's neck and softly cooed, "The secrets of the planet are whispered. They are no louder than a supple breeze or a calm sea. Go to the shore and pray to Pettr. Tell me later what you learn."

There was love, and there was trust. Lupé smiled and launched himself toward the surf.

The petrel came to his favorite spot. He positioned himself so that the wind was in his face. The sand and the sea covered his webbed feet, and the sun warmed his body. Just as he was about to begin, the petrel noticed someone on the rock next to him—Stithl.

"Yo, Lubé!" the iguana called. "Whudd'a goot mornin'." Then he crawled off the rock to be closer to his friend.

Lupé decided not to tell Stithl anything. He was very uncomfortable with how Stithl treated serious matters like love, romance, and nesting. *That's just the way reptiles are, so cold blooded. They can't help it*, Lupé conceded to himself. Still, he was determined not to mention Sirka. No good could come of it.

Unfortunately, Stithl had come to no such decision. The very first thing he asked was, "Why aren'd ya wid Sirgka an' ta groub? Whudd'a ya doin' here?"

Lupé kept it vague. He explained that there were some things on his mind and thought a little meditation might help. He hoped Stithl would take the hint and leave him to his thoughts, but "hint" was not a concept Stithl understood.

A sly reptilian grin creased the lumpy lizard's face as he asked, "Who wuz dad who visidet ya lassd nighd?"

Lupé said nothing.

Stithl continued, "I would'n've menshun'd id ad all, bud I live so glose, I gouldn'd helb bud nodice." This lizard's grin did not disappear. Rather, it grew tighter and more twisted.

"Id's jussd, well, ad firsd id loogk't da me ligke ya were in drouble. I dought'd ya mighd neet my helb, bud as I grawl't oud from unda my rogck . . . Well, Lubé, all I gan say iss dad id wuz obvious ya neetet no helb from me."

The petrel was not enjoying this at all, and that made it all the more enjoyable for Stithl.

"Ya know me, da lasd ding I't eve wanda to iss bry, bud dell me one ding, if ya will be so kint." At this point, it looked like Stithl was fighting to hold his grin in place, not to keep it from vanishing. He was trying to keep it from exploding. The iguana continued, "Wuz dad Sirgka I saw ya wid?"

It was obvious to Lupé that Stithl already knew the answer to that question and a whole lot more. It bothered the petrel so much, the way Stithl was playing with it, that he screeched, "How dare you, you cold-blooded, stone-sitting, landlocked lump of a lizard. This isn't something I care to discuss with some insincere algae eater who just crawled out from under a rock. Besides, I don't peck and tell."

"Goodn'd dad be begcause ya've neva agcdually pegck'd before? Bud ya dit lassd nighd, ditn'd ya?"

Lupé said nothing. The thought of being with Sirka was so strong, he reacted physically. He felt a warm satisfaction throughout his body. A new security and purpose filled what had once been empty within him. Lupé had a mate. She was real. They were real, and he would be with her again tonight, tomorrow . . . forever. When the petrel returned from his thoughts about Sirka, he found himself facing Stithl in a dreamy haze, grinning like a dolphin.

It was all Stithl needed to see. His question was answered.

Then the lizard made a strange request. He said, "When ya see Dabao, magke sure ya dell `im dad you an' Sirgka'r nesdin' ub tugetha."

Lupé did not bother denying the development. Stithl knew, and that was that. Instead, Lupé explained that he wasn't sure how Tapao would react to the news. So it might not be such a good idea to just land next to the Darum leader and blurt out, "By the way, your niece and I are nesting."

The iguana emitted a wheezing snicker and said, "Jussd dell `im, he'll be habby."

"That's a nice thought," Lupé replied, "but I'm not so sure that's how it will go."

"Drussd me, Dabao won'd be ubbsed."

Lupé hated false confidence, especially when the source of it had nothing to lose.

Stithl continued, "An' when ya dell Dabao, remint `im dad he owes me twendy glams . . . oben't."

"Why would Tapao owe you twenty clams?"

"Id'z a nesdin' presend."

"But I'm the one who's nesting," the petrel said.

Stithl nodded. "An dad's why he owes me dwendy oben't glams."

Now Lupé knew why the lizard was so confident Tapao would approve of the mating. He had paid Stithl to help it happen.

But before he could give the corrupt reptile the lambasting he deserved, the iguana said, "Loogk, Lubé . . . if I tawd I wuz goin' da be involve't wid someding dad would hurd ya, I would't neva `ve wend along wid Dabao. Bud ya love Sirgka, an' she loves ya' bagck. Dabao an' I knew dad a long dime ago. We jussd helb't ya bo't realize id. An' neet'a of us force't ya ta do anytin'. Ya habby. Sirgka's habby. Dabao'll be habby. So whud's da harm if I ged dwendy glams for spreatin' a liddle habbiness?"

Stithl suddenly stopped. He creased his already creased brow, twisted his already twisted mouth, and raised his tail. The lizard grinned at Lupé and said, "Maybe I bedda assgk fa' fiddy. Whudd'a ya dingk? Dings really dit worgk oud nice." With that, Stithl strode away, lost in thought, planning his renegotiation.

Lupé was amazed at how unpredictable the creatures on Galahope were. *They may be strange,* he thought, *but they are kinda fun.* He could not deny that he was happy to be with Sirka. And if Stithl was correct, which was a big if, Tapao would be happy too. So it seemed all was well—everyone was pleased.

The surf that broke near Lupé grew more lively as it rushed over his legs, shaking him. A thick band of white covered the shallow shoreline, foaming and bubbling where the sea struck rock and sand. Lupé scanned the horizon. A dark figure broke through the clouds and plummeted from the gray sky. Lupé's initial reaction was to think *hawk*. And then he knew. It was a Darum, the one who would not be happy with the news.

The Darum dove with the sun fully behind him, hoping the glare would keep Lupé from noticing the attack. It was something hawks often did, a technique Kurah had taught his son to spot long ago. Lupé had also learned that an approach like this meant only one thing. There would be no talk. Bog had death in his heart.

For a moment, Lupé thought he would fly up to meet Bog in the sky. He knew Bog did not have the skill to fly with him, but even if they did battle on the wing, the fight would ultimately be decided on land. That was where the final blow would fall. Lupé understood that only one bird would fly away from this encounter. And he was going to make sure it was a Gwatta.

Lupé prepared himself within. On the outside, he stood as though he were deep in prayer. He let Bog continue thinking the attack would be a surprise. And with Bog virtually on top of him, Lupé bounced to one side, caught his attacker's beak with his own, and drove it down into the ground. When Bog's beak caught the sand, his momentum was shattered. It flipped him over, and he struck the beach with his back.

Lupé gave his opponent one chance to reconsider, but the gesture was wasted.

As he rose to face Lupé, Bog screeched, "You will not plant your seed in my flock!" Then the Darum swept his wing along the ground, spraying the Gwatta with sand while he also fired a blast of oil at his enemy. When Lupé extended his wing to shield his eyes, Bog attacked. He shot in under the wing and grabbed Lupé's neck with his beak. Bog held his opponent by the throat while he crashed his relatively large body against the smaller petrel. Lupé's neck was being stretched and crushed at the same time. A closed beak slammed into Lupé's flank, another ripped at his leg, and yet another twisted his wing.

He wondered, "How many beaks does Bog have?" A better question would have been, "How many beaks does Bog command?" Others had arrived and joined Bog in tearing at the Gwatta. There was nothing Lupé could do. When he wriggled free from one, the others held him. When he popped into the air, they grabbed him and forced him down, and the beating intensified. At this rate, Lupé knew he could not last long.

The petrel needed help . . . and that's exactly what he got. From a rock overhead, Stithl threw himself onto the pecking pack. A moving mass of feathers, with an iguana draped over it, rolled down the shore into a small tidal pool.

By the time they splashed into the shallow water, Lupé was free from the tangle of attackers. When the others got to their feet, several popped into the air ready to resume the destruction of Lupé. But Stithl made them pause. He whipped one of the birds from the air with his tail. Lupé noticed and was happy the iguana's appendage grew back so quickly and so fully.

The Darums wanted to keep Lupé grounded so that he could not escape. But now they were faced with a problem. In order to keep Lupé from flying, they'd have to battle Stithl as well. Lupé had a deadly ally. Although he usually appeared quite slow and sluggish, when he wanted to, Stithl could be incredibly quick, striking with the flash and power of lightning.

The lizard stood high on his front and hind legs. He opened his jaws and angled his hard head while he hissed and snapped at the petrels. The reptile knew how to fight and was ready to go the distance.

For the most part, Bog's companions were terrified. Stithl made sure no other thought entered their little minds. He grabbed the bird he had plucked from the sky. When he had the Darum in his jaws, he rolled his own body with an abrupt, violent twist, his own riff on a crocodile's death roll, snapping the petrel's wing like a dry twig. This was one Darum who would never fly again. It presented a possibility that did not appeal to his comrades. They understood exactly what Stithl was telling them.

The lizard released the bird and called to Lupé, who was still occupied with his own battle. "I can gkeeb `em away, bud ya'll hav-da teal wid Bog yasef."

Which is precisely what Lupé did. He and Bog wrestled, scraped, and bit until they broke free from each other. They faced off, petrel to petrel. Bog slid his crooked, chipped beak back and forth slowly. A grating click cut through the air. Then Bog said, "You are what's left of a dead flock, Gwatta. I will not allow us to become in-fested with your weakness."

Lupé answered, "As the last of my flock, aren't I also the stron-gest?"

"But I am the strongest of both our flocks. You are the end waiting to happen. And now is the time."

Lupé did not move. He wasn't sure what to do next, so he de-cided to wait for Bog to strike. If his opponent made a mistake or a foolish decision, Lupé would take advantage.

"Now I will remove you from this island, and I will remove the Gwattas from this Earth." With that, Bog spread his wings, shot a stream of hot oil at Lupé, and charged. Lupé flapped once and lifted himself above the attack. Bog looked up. He was prepared to crush whatever part of Lupé he could catch with his beak. And when the Darum opened his mouth to bite, Lupé closed his own beak tightly and rammed his head down into Bog's throat.

It looked as though Bog had swallowed Lupé, and his follow-ers thought that's exactly what happened. They were so excited with the victory they began planning an attack on Stithl. Then Bog started to gag. He could not breathe. The Darum tried to shake Lupé from within him, but the smaller petrel would not let go. He responded by burying his beak deeper inside Bog's throat. One of them would suffocate before the other.

Occasionally, a petrel slipped past Stithl and went straight for Lupé, cuffing and biting his exposed body. But Lupé was so fo-cused, he did not hear Stithl's warnings or feel the Darum's blows. Although Bog lifted the smaller petrel off the ground, it seemed the Gwatta was gaining control.

When he felt Bog finally fall to the ground, limp, Lupé withdrew. Whether Bog was dead or alive did not matter. Lupé had proved his point. But before he could think another thought or take a much-needed breath, several Darums attacked.

Lupé and Stithl battled the birds, but more arrived. There were now too many for Stithl to control himself, although he continued to try. Lupé knew he no longer had the strength to defeat them. There were so many, and he had beaten their leader so severely, he believed that Bog's followers would surely execute him. Every part of his body was being pecked, pulled, tugged, twisted, and torn.

Still, Lupé fought on. He would not give his life away. It would have to be taken from him. And when it seemed that would be the petrel's fate, something strange happened. There weren't so many attackers to fight off. Bog's companions were being driven away.

Sirka had returned with her group of fishers, who were delighted to see how they could apply their fine flying skills to battle. Many of the youngsters were overjoyed at another realization: they were now as large as Bog's cohorts. But for a bird to be successful in battle, it needs speed as well as size. Sirka's group had grown strong and quick fishing at sea, while Bog's followers had grown heavy and slow foraging for jellyfish and clams.

Yip, Kelp, Sirka, and others beat Lupé's attackers mercilessly until they retreated from the fight. When Wohat and the last few Darums would not release Lupé, Sirka swooped by and lowered her heels into Wohat's head, pecking at his face to add emphasis. Immediately, several of the pupils mimicked their instructor as if it was some feeding technique they were supposed to practice on Wohat's head.

Soon, Lupé was free, and his assailants were gone. Even Bog dragged himself along the shore as he limped off alone . . . well, not completely alone. Yip and Kelp followed him, pecking, diving, cuffing, and shooting him with blasts of hot oil just to help Bog remember the day a little better.

Sirka escorted Lupé and Stithl back to the nest. The iguana's tough hide had protected him well. Occasionally, he stopped to cough up loose feathers. Several hung from the corners of his mouth. The lizard never bothered to wipe them off. He wore them with pride.

Lupé had not fared quite as well as his lumpy friend. The petrel could not fly and had trouble walking, although he would admit neither. Instead, he whispered to Sirka, "It would be rude to fly home and leave Stithl to walk alone after what he just did for me."

Sirka could see Lupé dragging a limp wing through the sand. It left a crease in the sand alongside his footprints as he tried to catch up to the iguana.

In the clouds above the trio, youngsters from the group flew watch. Even with Bog incapacitated, they were taking no chances and waited to see that their friends were not ambushed by those who escaped the battle.

Stithl suddenly sniffed deeply and then vanished over the hill that led to his rocky lair. When Lupé and Sirka heard a long, loud, "Haaahhh!" they were sure the reptile had finally collapsed. But when the pair climbed over the sand expecting to see the worst, they found Stithl with his head buried in an immense clam.

The sticky, smelly brine dripped down his neck while he sucked out the soft meat. Stithl was surrounded by a hundred cracked clams. It appeared Tapao had paid his debt, with a generous bonus. The petrels heard nothing but intense slurping and an occasional, "I love Dabao," from the hungry lizard.

Sirka didn't understand where the clams had come from and what Tapao had to do with them. Leaving Stithl to enjoy his reward, Lupé's only comment was, "I'll tell you all about it later."

Back at the nest, the pair was greeted by Yip, Kelp, and a finch named Wiff. Wiff was a strange bird—large for his kind, but much smaller and faster than any of the petrels. He was a very smart finch who had an unusual preoccupation: he spent almost all his time talking to sick birds, no matter what flock they were from.

Ill birds were usually avoided by anyone outside of the family. Most believed it was up to Pettr to decide who lived and who died. But Wiff actually sought these birds out, studied them, and tried to help them. He would sit up all night and gather strange foods or instruct them to do weird things.

Many of those who followed Wiff's advice improved quickly. He seemed to know more about healing than any creature on the island. And he seemed to carry Pettr's blessing. No petrel or hawk, no lizard or seal would ever harm Wiff. They knew how important he could be.

Although Wiff was genuinely upset any time he saw a creature in pain, he never pressured any bird to take his advice. He would offer it, and you could do as you wished. Wiff asked Lupé if it would be all right to examine him. *Sirka* said it would be welcome.

While Lupé was being poked and prodded—only a touch more gently than he had experienced at the beak of Bog and his cohorts—Yip and Kelp offered some interesting information. They were on Bog's tail, quite literally, when the defeated Darum returned to the colony.

Tapao was waiting. He approached Bog and said, "Petrels cannot fly with only one wing. Both wings must surrender to the idea; likewise, one must be totally devoted to the flock . . . totally devoted to flying the good flight . . . And you are not."

It was understood that Tapao had not taken part in the earlier fight, and it was also understood that Bog and his gang were lucky he stayed out of it. Tapao was undeniably older, but he was absolutely a warrior. The leader went on to strip Bog of all his rank and responsibility. Since he had never commanded their respect, and since they were no longer afraid of him, Bog also lost most of his influence over the Darums who flew at his side.

"And," Yip screeched, "Tapao made the totally glide choice of placing two proper petrels—namely, us—in charge of flock security!" The brother and sister were so excited, they burst into the air and flew spirals around each other, trying to work off their emotion.

Watching the display, Sirka said, "Security might become a little lax around here, but we're gonna have a lot more fun." In between Lupé's ouching and ooing, he and Sirka congratulated their former pupils. The pair decided it was time to form a new group with younger birds and start all over. Things were changing.

Time passed. Winds blew, rains fell, tides rose and then crept back into the sea. Whether it happened that first night under the moon or whether it happened some other, there was no escaping it . . . Sirka was pregnant—so much so that many of the petrels were concerned for her health, not the least of which was Lupé.

They were worried about Sirka, because she had grown so large, it didn't seem healthy. Wiff was a constant visitor to the nest. The finch confessed to Lupé that he had never seen swelling like Sirka's before, not in any bird. Even Lupé knew that female petrels always laid a single egg, which accounted for roughly half their body weight. Sirka, however, had expanded well beyond that. She could not fly and even had difficulty walking. It was getting so bad, she reminded Lupé of a cute, clean . . . Zomis.

Whenever Sirka slept, Lupé dismantled a section of the nest and made it a little larger. He hoped his mate would not notice how big she was getting, but she did. And the closer Sirka came to egg-laying, the larger she got. Lupé worried that the pregnancy might cost his mate her life and that he was to blame.

The idea of losing her terrified him. It was one thing to go through life alone, but how could he cope with losing the one bird he had searched so long to find? Others had been taken from him, but Sirka was different. They were one. Lupé knew the only thing to do was give Sirka the best care he could.

That, however, was easier said than done. There were others also trying to take care of Sirka. Yip and Kelp, Wiff, Stithl, the current group of young fishers, the graduates from past groups, parents, and others all wanted to do what they could for Sirka. Tapao pretended not to be concerned, but more than once, the Darum leader was caught fluffing Sirka's nest, dropping off food, and asking the youngsters how his niece was doing.

For Lupé, the only peace he got was when he took the young-sters out to sea. There were usually fewer birds in the fishing group than there were hovering around his home attending to Sirka. Nev-er was a bird more pampered or cared for. For both Lupé and Sirka, the attention was heartwarming, but it was also annoying.

As uncomfortable as her pregnancy and all the attention made Sirka feel, she remained in good spirits. Lupé told Stithl that life with her was like flying with a tailwind. She was an effortless com-panion who only had to be herself to make life wonderful for her mate. Even though Sirka was quick to laugh at her predicament, Lupé could see beneath the good humor. He could tell that Sirka ached at her inability to fly, wondered whether she'd live or die . . . and worried about losing the life within her.

Lupé did his best to comfort his mate, but it was a difficult task to accomplish with so many others around the nest set on the same purpose. At times, when the Darum nest-flies wouldn't let Lupé get close to his mate, he would sneak away to pray, to listen to the si-lence that often gave answers. Sometimes Lupé would meditate on the wing, soaring above the sea. It reminded him of migration, when one was forced to pray while flying. It also reminded him of being alone, with only Sirka beside him. During these solitary moments, Lupé prayed that Sirka and their egg would both be healthy.

Even though it seemed his mate might lay her egg that very afternoon, when several Darums showed up at his nest and the breeze began to tug at his feathers, Lupé seized the opportunity to make a quick flight around the island. Seduced by the wind, Lupé answered its call.

He reflected on Sirka's eyes as he flew. Dark and wet, they al-ways reassured and comforted Lupé with their warm sparkle. It was as if there was something behind the eyes, a knowledge or con-fidence that whatever happened, as long as Lupé and Sirka were to-gether, all would be well. Lupé wondered whether his mate saw the same thing in his eyes. Sirka and her inner glow were now part of Lupé's life, a part he did not want to lose.

Lupé thought of their egg. It was the egg that caused Sirka's difficulty. Even if all went well, if Sirka survived and the egg hatched, what would they find? Was the chick that caused her to swell diseased . . . dead? And what if this birth ended Sirka's ability to conceive others? These were frightening thoughts. The wind whispered and stroked Lupé's wings, reminding him that whatever happened was Pettr's will and that time would answer all his questions.

Gliding over a supple stretch of sea, Lupé's attention was drawn to the translucent reflection of a jellyfish floating below. The petrel decided a snack was in order and swooped toward his food. With ease, he lifted the lumbering morsel from the blue. He swallowed hard as he returned to the clouds.

Lupé swallowed a second time and realized that this jellyfish did not taste like any he had ever eaten before. It was soft, but it was also hard. It could be chewed, but it did not fall apart in his beak. It slid partway down the petrel's throat and lodged there. Lupé began to gag and gasp. He could neither swallow nor dislodge the strange thing. It was choking him.

Whatever it was, Lupé knew this was no jellyfish. It felt and looked like clear, durable seaweed. He was reminded of something Stithl told the group when the iguana spoke about scavenging the shoreline. "All dad glidduhs is nod fooot." Was this what the lizard was talking about? Lupé became concerned. He was not taking in enough air—less with every breath. He had to get to shore and clear his throat before he suffocated.

Lupé wondered if he was going to join Pettr before Sirka . . . if he and his mate would leave a parentless egg. Lupé was crushed with the thought that he might father a chick who was more alone than him. He knew if he didn't tend to the problem at wing, at the very least, his egg would be hatched without a father. Lupé struggled to reach the shore while the thing that strangled him sank deeper into his throat.

Back at the nest, Sirka was struggling as well. She fought to thrust the enormous egg from within her body. Tapao, Stithl, Wiff, and the others waited to see what would emerge, what it was that birdened Sirka so.

Lupé's mate pushed hard and felt a stab of pain that went beyond the pain of birth. It was as if something reached into her abdomen and clawed at her soul. Immediately, her thoughts flew to Lupé. Where was he? She cawed his name and heard no answer.

Lupé made it to shore. He would not drown, but he was by no means out of danger. Few would have noticed the solitary bird watching from above the clouds, but as Lupé stood on the rocks choking, he could see Bog circling high overhead. Looking more like a vulture than a petrel, Bog swooped down and landed just a flap away from his dying adversary.

Lupé was as helpless as a fish washed up on the sand. The choking petrel did not move. He found that if he took delicate, short breaths, he could take in some air and still keep the weed from sliding further down his throat. A small piece hung from the corner of Lupé's beak, a piece just long enough for another petrel to grab. He wondered whether Bog would seize the opportunity to kill him or rise above their past and pull the killer seaweed from his enemy's throat. Either choice would result in the end of hostility between the two birds.

Bog hopped closer to Lupé and watched, expressionless. There was no compassion in his face, no mercy, no love in his eyes. Bog leaned forward, tilted his head, took one last look, and flew off, leaving Lupé to die.

From the day he was hatched, Lupé knew he owed the Creator a death. It was, perhaps, the most un-mysterious thing about life . . . one day it would end. But Lupé hoped his death was not being collected now. He had come too far to lose it all so foolishly.

Lying against the wet rocks on the threshold of forever, Lupé thought of his flock, his family, and his mate. He began to chant *Sea, Sun, Soil* over and over to himself. It was a final, desperate attempt to call Pettr. The lack of oxygen made Lupé dizzy. It felt as if the shore was spinning, tumbling. He couldn't control the feeling, and he didn't know whether it was the waves, the wind, or his demise that caused the sensation.

Soon, Lupé was looking down at the shore. He had left himself behind. He could see his body draped over the gray rocks, motionless, lifeless. His neck was stretched and contorted. From the corner of his beak hung the imposter jellyfish that strangled him.

The feathered speck on the beach that only moments earlier had contained his essence was now nothing but an empty shell, like so many others waiting for the tide to wash them away. Soon, the beach also became a speck . . . and then the island . . . and then . . .

Like vapor evaporating off the sea, Lupé drifted up through white clouds. He felt as though he was becoming part of the sky, blending into the blue, moving effortlessly toward the life of the planet as he was pulled by the silent strength of the sun. The sky was so big and he was so small, Lupé felt absorbed by its vastness. He was nothing. The sky that carried clouds, wind, rain, and birds now carried a spirit, perhaps the Gwatta's last life.

And then it came to him. The final word of the savn mantra was *Sky*. Lupé repeated it over and over to himself—*Sea, Sun, Soil, Sky . . . Sea, Sun, Soil, Sky*—but it was too late. He knew his life on Pettr's Earth, his life with Sirka and the Darums, was over. As he drifted closer to the burning eye, he saw the searing white but still could not feel the heat.

Something flapped and flashed across the fiery orb, a black silhouette against bright white. It looked like . . . a bird.

Lupé continued to drift closer and closer to Pettr's burning eye. He wondered what it was that flew so close to the sun. He wondered whether he would pass through or be consumed in the fire that filled the sky. Soon, he would know whether or not he had flown the good flight. He continued the chant as he floated on.

The dark little bird appeared again . . . flapped, fluttered, hovered, and then flew off.

Lupé was confused. He had no idea where the mysterious creature came from. He knew of no bird that flew at this height or in this sky. Although puzzled, he wasn't afraid. Lupé actually had the feeling the bird liked him. "Either way," he reasoned, "what can happen to me now? I'm already dead. The only thing left is the sun."

Lupé's thoughts soared to Sirka. If she survived the birthing, she would have to raise their chick without her mate. Even if he was permitted to pass through Pettr's eye, to go where the many fly as one, Lupé thought he would never be happy. No matter what the other side was like, there could be no happiness without Sirka. He could never be Lupé unless she was with him. He knew he would wait patiently for the day Sirka came to join him. But his thoughts assumed that both he and Sirka would be allowed to join Pettr.

Lupé turned to the sun and began to feel the heat that awaited him, but with subtle swiftness he was surrounded by a cool white mist that obstructed Pettr's burning eye. He could no longer feel the searing heat as he floated in an ocean of clouds. Lupé knew that he was moving, but he had no idea what carried him or where it was taking him.

Then Lupé saw her, a petrel from his flock. There was no doubt about it. She looked exactly like those he remembered, and she carried the scent of the Gwattas. She was younger than Lupé, incredibly agile on the wing, and beautiful.

As she studied Lupé, the feathers on the back of her neck stood with curiosity. She smiled and flew closer. There was something familiar about this bird, something that went beyond her look and smell.

Lupé wondered, "Is she real? Am I real?" She was near enough to touch. Lupé reached out a wing from the body he thought he left empty on the beach. It brushed the female lightly. When they touched, a jolt of heat charged through Lupé. It made him feel alert and strong, as if the other petrel poured power directly into his body.

The female giggled. She laid her head directly against his and whispered, "Hello, Lupé."

If he didn't know her, she certainly knew him. All the faces of all the females he had ever met from his flock raced through Lupé's mind. It didn't take long. There weren't that many. This face, however, did not appear in his mind's eye. Judging from her appearance, she couldn't have been more than a hatchling when they had met. Faces could change as young mature. Still, Lupé could not place this petrel. She was familiar, but he could not identify her.

Again, the female whispered. This time, she said, "Hello, Grandson."

Something inside Lupé told him to believe what this bird suggested. How could he, though? To believe her, he would have to believe that his grandmother was half his age. But the longer he looked at her, the more convinced he became. *Yes*, Lupé finally admitted, *she is Pakeet.*

The beautiful, young . . . grandmother ignored Lupé's gaping and said, "Barau watches you very closely. He told me you were coming . . . Your brother misses you."

"Barau?" It sounded so strange to hear the name again. "Is Barau with you?" Lupé asked.

"He is near," Pakeet replied.

Lupé was flooded with questions, but the first one to cross his beak was, "Mother and Father, are they with you and Barau?"

"We are all together on the other side."

"Then we are not on the other side right now?"

"Not yet."

"When can I see them?" the anxious petrel pleaded.

"We will decide that now . . . It is why I am here." Pakeet's tone grew more urgent when she said, "There is something I must explain to you . . . As long as our flock remains on the planet, we are able to watch and maybe someday return in the feathers of another. But if our line ends, the souls of the flock die with it. We will no longer see. And we will never return. Although we are not certain, you are likely the last Gwatta. If you pass through Pettr's eye, it could be the end."

"What can I do? I might be the last Gwatta, but I'm not the last *living* Gwatta, not anymore."

Pakeet studied her grandson, weighing the words she was about to speak. Again, the feathers on the back of her neck lifted themselves. "You have flown the good flight. I have seen. You will pass through. You can join your parents, Barau, the rest of the flock, me, on the other side . . . or I can send you back."

"*You can send me back*?!" Lupé screeched. "Back to Sirka . . . Back to Galahope?"

"Yes, it seems I can."

"Then send me," Lupé said without hesitation.

Pakeet nodded, indicating that she understood and that Lupé should not rush her. She said, "Understand this, Grandson. If you return and do not continue to fly the good flight, the next time you approach the sun, you will not make it through. And I will not be able to send you back a second time."

"You're sure I will pass through this time?"

"Yes."

Lupé thought for a moment, long enough to consider Kurah, Raza, Barau . . . He thought about Pakeet and the others he had known who were now gone from his life. But when he considered Sirka and their unborn chick, Lupé knew.

"Send me back," he said. "I want to raise my young—your young." He looked above, beyond the mist. "The flock's young."

Pakeet cautioned, "I am not sure your young will keep us connected to the planet. Their mother is not one of us."

"What difference does that make?" Lupé challenged defensively.

"Maybe no difference at all. Maybe a great deal. I am not criticizing Sirka. She is a special bird. But she is not a Gwatta. Just father your family, Lupé, and we will see what happens. We will see if the love you and Sirka share is enough to save the Gwattas."

"Before I go," Lupé said, "I would like to see Barau."

"You have already seen him, and he has seen you. The little one you saw flying across the sun, that was your brother. You cannot get any closer or speak to him. Kurah and Raza also want to see you, but you are being given an unusual opportunity. If you make contact with anyone other than me, you will have to join us right now. With Pettr's blessing, we will all be able to greet you when you return to us. Believe me, the time will come soon enough."

"Tell them I love them and miss them."

Pakeet nodded, "They know." She paused and added, "We are watching. We are with you."

"Will you tell Barau, I'm sorry. It is my fault he lost his life. I was—"

"It is not your fault. There is no forgiveness to ask. Barau is happy. He's in a better place, and one day you will join him."

Lupé flashed a suggestive grin, the kind Stithl was known for, and said, "I will tell Tapao you said hello."

Now it was Pakeet's turn to smile. She said, "You will not, because you will not remember. But I may tell him myself someday."

Lupé nodded. "Send me back."

Pakeet stood tall on the mist. She said, "You are savn. You know the words. Say them."

Her grandson obeyed.

Then Pakeet said, "Return to your nest and see what has happened." The beautiful, young grandmother reached out and touched Lupé once more.

Another hot blast burned through his body. He shook violently and felt as though he had pecked at lightning. Then Lupé slipped from the warm wind and the cool clouds of eternity.

The petrel could feel his heart beating but could not yet move. He forced unfocused eyes to open and couldn't believe what he thought he saw. The hard jellyfish that strangled him was slowly being tugged from his mouth. It was being pulled out by an old friend, the butterfly. But suddenly the butterfly flew off, leaving the death in Lupé's throat. Once again, the petrel began to suffocate.

Lupé heard the noise that had startled the monarch. They were steps. Something was coming closer. And then Lupé saw what it was. He could see the two large feet approaching, the same feet that had gathered the rodents from the jaws. It was a human. Lupé wondered what would finish him first: the choking, or the cruel featherless fingers of the man-flock. He was strangely amused at how far he had flown, only to die like this.

Then he felt them. He was wrapped in them, lifted from the sand and held tight. It was horrible, and Lupé was powerless. Once again he was being held. Two fingers pinched his beak open. Lupé gagged. *There is no escaping the man-flock*, he thought.

He felt it. The hard, clear jellyfish or seaweed, whatever it was that choked him, was slowly tugged from his throat. A finger gently ran down Lupé's nape. He was lowered back onto the sand and the two huge feet trudged on down the beach. Sitting in a massive footprint was the smiling butterfly.

Laying in the sand, Lupé took a deep breath and tasted the air of Galahope once more. His throat was clear, and so was his vision. The deadly weed was gone. The tender touch of the unseen had returned Lupé to his body and placed him back inside Pettr's. He was born again.

The petrel stood and paced off a few steps. He felt fine, so he launched himself into the air and flew to Sirka.

Arriving at his nest, Lupé was never so happy to see Stithl, Tapao, Yip, Kelp, Wiff, and several other Darums hovering around his home. More than anything else, he was relieved to see Sirka. She was in good health and everyone was excited—so excited, in fact, they never even asked Lupé where he had been. No one cared.

The pair was faced with a new concern. The birth had gone well, too well. Sirka had borne the burden admirably, managing to do something none of the petrels had ever seen before: she had laid two eggs. They were white, slightly oblong, and looked to be quite healthy. Tiny red speckles appeared near the wider ends.

Lupé was astounded and overjoyed. The same was true for the others, who were busy arguing what the two youngsters would look like when they hatched. The proud Gwatta did not hesitate to join the conversation.

It was one thing to hear Tapao and Lupé gloat over the phemonena of twin eggs and then boast about personal features the youngsters would be "lucky" to inherit, but when Stithl began to insist that the chicks could possess some reptilian qualities, Sirka had enough. That was when the young mother demanded all visitors leave her and her mate to their new family.

When the pair was finally alone, Sirka was faced with another dilemma: Which egg would she sit on? She looked to the new father and said, "Since you had as much to do with this as me, fluff up your rump and pick one."

At first, instinct told Lupé to protest, to remind his mate that he was supposed to fly out to sea and return with food, but as he looked at the magnificent eggs before him and thought about the helpless lives within, he was honored to join Sirka. To be able to hatch his own young was a dream come true.

Lupé watched Sirka sit carefully down on one of the eggs. He fluffed himself exactly as he had seen her do. And when he was just about to cover the other egg, he realized another had beaten him to it, the one visitor who had not left. The speckled egg was protected by the outstretched wings of the old egg-sitter himself, the butterfly. Lupé's silent friend had followed him back from the other side and apparently decided to stay for a while. This time, however, the eggs beneath the butterfly's tiny rump were not robin's eggs, they were petrel eggs, new life for a desperate flock.

Lupé grinned, looked up to the clouds, and breathed deep. Pettr's air tasted sweet.

The End

Author's Note

Several of the characters described in this story fall into one of these categories: threatened, endangered, or extinct. The characters reflect actual species, and most of their habits and habitats depict basic realities.

In the language of the man-flock, Lupé's species is known as the Guadalupe Island Petrel (the Gwattas in the text). Once found in the Pacific (or the Ocean of Peace) off the coast of Mexico, the last Guadalupe Petrel was seen in 1911. Their complete demise is attributed to the introduction of rats, cats, dogs, and pigs to their fragile habitat by some careless human visitors.

These non-indigenous predators ravaged the ground nesting populations of petrels, who were not equipped to cope with the rapid change in their once stable world. Although globally a few species of petrels that were once listed as extinct have re-appeared, that has not been the case for Lupé's flock. They seem to be gone, wiped out somewhat accidentally by man, underscoring how fragile life on Earth can be.

If you haven't already guessed, the Islands of Life (aka Galahope) are the Galapagos Islands off the coast of Ecuador. The flock that Lupé adopts, the Darums, really do maintain a colony there and are known to the man-flock as Hawaiian Dark-rumped Petrels. They are an endangered species fighting to survive, and humans are, in fact, helping in that effort.

Another imperiled creature that appears in the story is Gilgongo and Pingolo, Green Sea Turtles. These turtles are listed as "endangered," as are all species of sea turtles—all of them. The Green, which is actually more brown or tan than green, is in jeopardy mainly due to beach development which has destroyed their traditional nesting grounds, excessive predation of the young, and indiscriminant netting from fishing boats.

But there are other factors that take a toll on these marine reptiles. Trash floating on the sea that masquerades as food, poor water quality, unsecured fishing tackle, collisions with motorboats and jet skis, as well as natural predators that would normally reduce healthy populations, all contribute to a decline in sea turtles across the planet.

Finally, I claimed literary license to resurrect another extinct species besides the Guadalupe Petrel . . . Zomis. Even though he might not realize it, Zomis is no ordinary pigeon. He is a Passenger Pigeon, another bird that became extinct in the early 1900s.

At this point, all I can say is that I wish it was as easy to bring extinct creatures back to life on the planet as it is on the page. And I hope that when I write the story of Lupé's and Sirka's chicks there won't be too many new characters to add to the cast of extinct, endangered, and threatened creatures and habitats.

Acknowledgments

Lupé and I would like to thank . . .

Kris and the boys for their patience, good humor, and thoughtful suggestions.

John Sawhill for his inspiration, his example, and his contribution.

Mark Tercek and the Nature Conservancy family for their incredible work and example. Also to Mark for leading what is often a struggle to protect and preserve the natural wonders of this world. And for taking time to pen the Introduction. It's a deep honor to have this story associated with the Nature Conservancy.

Jason Aydelotte, and all the Geckos, for bringing me and my work into their fold and for being a publisher of deep ethical conviction with regard to stories and their authors, something that should never be edited out of the publishing process.

Sarah Anderson for making "above and beyond" an everyday occurrence and for making images confined to one's mind take flight on the page for everyone to share.

To Josh Mitchell for such a complete understanding of what I was trying to produce and for being so adept at making gentle editing choices that lift the text where it needs to be.

Antha Adkins for such a comprehensive, detailed, and serious edit of the work.

Hilary Comfort for shepherding the editing process in such a professional way.

Monmouth University for giving a writer a wonderful home and for generous and consistent support.

Family, friends, colleagues, students, and, of course, readers for helping *A Wing and a Prayer* soar.

About the Author

John is a Professor of Journalism at Monmouth University in New Jersey. He studied at Clark University, Penn State University, and Adelphi University. John began his writing career in New York at *Modern Screen Magazine*, the nation's oldest movie magazine, where he served as lead film critic and managing editor. From there he moved to Los Angeles to become the founding editor-in-chief of *ROCKbeat Magazine* before returning to New York to become senior editor for *Inside Books Magazine*.

After years of covering the entertainment industry, as an academic John became interested in environmental issues and penned his first novel *A Wing and a Prayer*. With the success of his first book, *The John Morano Eco-Adventure Series* was born, and several more eco-adventure novels ensued.

John's work has been endorsed by The Nature Conservancy, World Wildlife Fund, Ocean Conservancy, ASPCA, and other world-class environmental organizations. He has been cited for making complex environmental issues accessible to a wide variety of readers in an entertaining, uplifting way. Professor Morano is also the author of *Don't Tell Me the Ending!*, a popular how-to textbook for aspiring film critics.

John lives in New Jersey on the northern tip of the Pine Barrens in a log home with his wife, two sons, and two rescued Australian Shepherds. When he's not writing or in the classroom, John can be found hiking streams in the woods and collecting Cretaceous fossils or, when his knees let him, running up and down the basketball court.

Connect with John

EMAIL:	morano@monmouth.edu
FACEBOOK:	www.facebook.com/EcoAdventureSeries
WEB:	www.johnmorano.com

About the Illustrator

Sarah E. Anderson is a visual artist who works primarily in 2D media such as painting, drawing, and printmaking. Her primary mediums include acrylics and pen and ink. She is also very interested in book making and graphic narratives.

Sarah has earned a bachelor's degree in Fine Arts from Carnegie Mellon University. She has also studied at the Pennsylvania Academy of Fine Arts in Philadelphia, and the Ecole nationale supe'rieure des Beaux-Arts in Paris, France.

She currently splits her time between Kutztown, PA and Pittsburgh, PA and is working toward a graduate degree in occupational therapy at Ohio State University in Columbus, Ohio. Her other interests include expanding her already large book collection, playing a variety of video games, attending philharmonic concerts, and running around the neighborhood.

Sarah would like to thank John Morano for giving her the opportunity to work on this book with him. She would also like to thank her parents for their continuing support.

Connect with Sarah

EMAIL: seandersonart@gmail.com

WEB: seandersonart.com

Support Indie Authors
& Small Press

If you liked this book, please take a few moments to leave a review on your favorite website, even if it's only a line or two. Reviews make all the difference to indie authors and are one of the best ways you can help support our work.

Reviews on Amazon, GreyGeckoPress.com, GoodReads, Barnes and Noble, or even on your own blog or website all help to spread the word to more readers about our books, and nothing's better than word-of-mouth!

http://smarturl.it/review-wing

Grey Gecko Press

Thank you for reading this book from Grey Gecko Press, an independent publishing company bringing you great books by your favorite new indie authors.

Be one of the first to hear about new releases from Grey Gecko: visit our website and sign up for our New Release or All-Access email lists. Don't worry: we hate spam, too. You'll only be notified when there's a new release, we'll never share your email with anyone for any reason, and you can unsubscribe at any time.

At our website you can purchase all our titles, including special and autographed editions, preorder upcoming books, and find out about two great ways to get free books, the Slushpile Reader Program and the Advance Reader Program.

And don't forget: all our print editions come with the ebook free!

Recommended Reading

Horse
by Leon Berger

This bittersweet chronicle of a working horse finally gaining his freedom was inspired by a real animal and true events, yet its underlying theme is about the universal value of friendship.

The hero is a sturdy draft horse: old, eccentric, and irritable. His name, suitably enough, is Groucho. By day, he hauls a tourist carriage around the heritage streets of Montreal. By night, he goes home to a stable in a run-down, working-class district.

When his owner dies, Groucho feels the loss and is helped through it by the ancient stableman, Doyle, who is also set in his ways. This is the story of how they cope with each other, as well as the threat which endangers their entire way of life.

amazon ☐iBooks
BARNES&NOBLE kobo

🦎 grey gecko press
http://bit.ly/141V9lW

Greystone Valley
by Charlie Brooks

Greystone Valley is a land of wizards, dragons, and warriors—and one young girl who goes there quite by accident when her idle wish is granted.

Sarah discovers that not everything in the valley is as magic as she might've wished—especially the nearly illiterate wizard, the mouse-sized dragon, and the warrior who can't stand the sight of blood. Being hunted isn't helping, either. Will Sarah survive this new life of hers, and can she make it home?

And, more importantly, can she ever be the same again?

amazon ☐iBooks
BARNES&NOBLE kobo

🦎 grey gecko press
http://bit.ly/1ehaBL8

CPSIA information can be obtained
at www.ICGtesting.com
Printed in the USA
BVHW072005231221
624644BV00004B/175